M000285319

bellicose press

Weather
Underwater

Kaisa Saarinen

First published in 2023 by Bellows Press

Copyright © Kaisa Saarinen, 2023

The author's rights are fully asserted. The rights of
Kaisa Saarinen to be identified as the author of this
work has been asserted by her in accordance with the
Copyright, Designs and Patents Act 1988

A CIP Catalogue of this book is available from
the British Library

ISBN: 978 1 739 71013 2

All rights reserved; no part of this publication may be reproduced,
stored in a retrieval system, or transmitted, in any form or by
any means, electronic, mechanical, photocopying, recording or
otherwise, without the prior written permission of the publisher.
Nor be circulated in any form of binding or cover other than that
in which it is published and a similar condition including this
condition being imposed on the subsequent purchaser.

Cover image
Alice M. @wildaltar

Cover design
Juliusz Grabianski @jgrab_ & Bart Seng Wen Long @antibart

Typeset by
Typo•glyphix
www.typoglyphix.co.uk

Printed and bound in England

For Kataja

In the absence
of weathermen

I'M WITH YOU in the water, holding you close and being embraced in kind by the true-blue night sky and the weight of the sea. Your body is soft, and I know all of it, every inch, better than you do. 'You're always too careless with yourself,' I whisper into your ear. Your head lolls against my shoulder, eyes closed, but I know you're listening. You're always listening to me. 'These bruises will take a long time to disappear. The cut from last week hasn't even healed yet.'

'They're nothing serious,' you mumble.

'They look ugly,' I say, although it's a lie. I only say it because I wish you'd stop getting into trouble; the little galaxies expanding on your smooth skin are lovely.

'I don't care about that. Matching my insides, I reckon.'

'You can be as ugly as you like, but I hate seeing you all banged up.' Those boys don't deserve to lay a finger on you. I caress a nasty cluster on the top of your left thigh and feel you wince against my collarbone. 'Should I not touch them?'

You shake your head, a small stubborn movement.

'What does that mean?'

'I want you to keep touching them.'

'Why? Doesn't it hurt?' I ask, tracing little butterfly patterns over the mauve constellation on your lower back.

'It does,' you whisper.

I keep caressing the bruised parts of you, keeping us upright in the cold waves. There are so many things I can't pronounce, but I know you're listening.

I love you.

Please stop fighting against everything that's not me.

Don't run away from me anymore.

You're so fucking stupid.

You mumble something against my skin, but your voice has gone too small to make out the words over the wind and the rush of water. Nobody else ever gets to hear your voice like this, and I want to keep it inside me and treasure it for the rest of my life,

So I do. It's still in my bones tonight, thrumming when I catch your bloodshot eyes, and my head swims with the weight of water from so many years ago. Your face makes me falter for a few seconds, becoming unfixed from the world, even as my legs tense up with the need to run away.

A cup of
flesh & bone

ELECTRIC MEDUSA, MIA thinks, staring down at a black tangle of cables underwater. Her vision is medically intact, yet badly blurred with a certainty of loss. The gleaming cords sway softly in the morning light, surrounded by the debris of skeletal bicycles, leather boots, a mass of things in indeterminate stages of decay. The sight of so much dead matter makes Mia feel overwhelmed with all the signs that she is alive – her body is throbbing a migraine beat, her nervous system awash with nauseating tides.

'What did they say to you?' she asks Rhys, who is kneeling by the water, staring at his pasty reflection.

'Not enough power to operate the extraction pump.' Rhys' eyes wander upwards, at the heaving sky. 'Besides, it's not over yet.'

'It's already fucked.'

'Must be about 50,000 people without power at present. Conservative estimate.'

'I'm aware.'

Neither of them mentions the number of houses submerged, of living beings washed away.

Rhys looks at Mia and smiles in that placid way of his. 'Look, it's out of our control. Whoever was in charge of sealing the terminations botched the job so badly, it's hard not to see it as sabotage.'

'I'm not looking for a scapegoat.'

'I'm just saying we don't need to beat ourselves up about this. Nobody can say we aren't doing our job. They've screwed us over.'

'Fine. I'm going back inside.' Mia brushes past Rhys and walks up the little hill to the substation control building.

She stands in the dim entryway, exhaling a hundred times, trying not to think about the infinite hunger of the river mouth – how it inhales guide dogs and garden sheds, midsummer roses and soft-bellied children. Mia walks into the kitchenette in the back and transfers some water from a yellow canister into a kettle. She sets one of the gas burners aflame and stands over the stove, listening to the liquid boil, cherishing the mundanity of that moment.

As soon as Mia sits down with her mug of tea, surrounded by the ringing silence of the room, bitter thoughts surge right through the barriers she so desperately tries to keep. There is so much anger brimming inside her, and nowhere for it to escape but in streams of tears down her cheeks, hot and shameful. Rhys comes in and thinks she must be sad; he is wrong, as usual. He doesn't say anything, but Mia can tell he feels *sorry* from the way he skulks around her, trying to make himself respectfully con-tained. *Fuck your condescension. Fuck you. Fuck you. Fuck you*, she thinks and takes a scalding sip of her tea. Rhys pours himself a fat finger of gin and retreats to his room, treasuring the glass with a two-handed grip. Mia hopes he won't get too drunk for too long. Now there is nothing to do but wait.

They have been working together for nearly three months, prisoners of the suburban substation damned to failure by their incompetent predecessors. The forced proximity has only widened the rift between them. The frequent blackouts they've been having

4

this summer, with no resources to fix anything quickly, are bad enough. The hostile atmosphere only adds minor insult to injury. Sometimes Mia wishes she could go back to that day she arrived in early March, make more of an effort to forge a connection with Rhys. In her heart, she knows this would only be possible if the change of timelines also involved a change in personalities. The things that bother her about Rhys haven't changed since the beginning, they were already evident in their first exchange.

'So you're from Portsmouth?'

'Yes.'

'I hope you don't mind me asking – how long have you been here for?'

'I evacuated six months ago.'

'You mean from Portsmouth?'

'Yes.'

'But what I'm trying to ask is where are you from originally?'

Mia had taken a deep breath and feigned confusion. *Boring. This is so fucking boring.* 'I was born in Gosport.' It was a half-truth, but she wasn't going to offer up any of her pain for him to mock.

The things the white boys in her class had said, after discovering why she was an orphan, were seared into her mind forever. 'You should've drowned with them.' 'Get back into the sea.'

'No offence, but you look like a refugee,' Rhys had said, nonchalant. Mia thought those boys must have grown up to be just like him.

'I *am* a refugee. From the south coast of England.'

'Come on, you know what I mean. You look like a Bengali on a boat.'

She had not uttered any of the insults that throbbed inside her head, desperate for release. She'd bitten the soft insides of her mouth until she tasted blood. The bluntest thing she has ever said to Rhys is,

'You make a habit of talking about things you have no direct experience of.' (The retort – 'Well, I've got an imagination. Haven't you?')

Maybe Mia has got it the wrong way around – it might be a blessing in disguise, having a ready source of irritation close at hand. It is a distraction, after all. There is a white noise of malaise in her head, looping every moment into a rosary of hopes undone. There must have been a time when she experienced life in a different way. Perhaps before she got on that evacuee train; before she graduated; before she knew how to mourn for the living and the dead. There must have been a time, but it was long ago, and this is the only state of being she knows. Hopelessness breeds a barren kind of fury, arid and cold and infinitely vast. Being mildly annoyed at another person is a very specific itch that one can scratch with silent curses, an oasis within her centreless anger.

The hostility of the outside is bleeding into the well-insulated substation control building. The rain batters against the roof, howling wind its loyal accompaniment. Mia's fingers twitch around the handle of the mug. Her mind thrums with the need to do something, to cut through the thick anticipation with the force of motion. Her body follows: she gets up and runs through the door, into the storm, down the little hill. Already the rain is infiltrating her eyes, turning them red and burning. She reaches the boundary of the river, three miles south of where it should be. The constellations of debris shift around as the liquid rises higher, still several inches below the concrete edge Mia is perched on.

She makes a cup of her open palms and bends down to fill it with filthy water. She raises her hands, lets the water spill on the porous surface of stone, and repeats this procedure six, twelve, twenty times. *Not enough power to operate the extraction pump*. What is this? She stills the motion of her hands, crosses them against her chest instead. She cries, and this time there is something like sadness in it too.

6

Moth in reverse

IT IS DIFFICULT to get used to waking up on dark summer mornings. The gentle sunlight that should stream in through the windows just isn't there. Neither are there shadows on the walls to follow with heavy eyelids, slowly taking in the shape of everything after long hours spent dreaming. Some mornings are still like that, yes, and Lily has learned to cherish them all the more. Sometimes the bright days come in pairs, or even longer sequences. During those stretches of time, it is easier to breathe; her body remembers how it used to be, before, when all July mornings were like this. Settling back into the old feeling of normality is a surprisingly quick and easy process. Stretching her limbs across the white bedsheets, touching her lover's cheek and keeping a tally of new freckles revealed by solar exposure. Especially after a string of mornings like that, the darkness always comes as a shock – not a whip-sharp pain but a dull thrum of anxiety settling into her bones. Anyone who has experienced compulsive violent thoughts will know the bliss of waking up with a blank mind and the horror of its transformation into a prison some seven seconds later. That is the mirror of this all-embracing darkness. Lily opens her eyes and immediately feels it settle into her bones, any grace period absent.

'Good morning,' Lily whispers into the pitch-black bedroom, heart beating fast and tight in her chest.

'Are you sure it's morning?' Joel says, his voice still raspy with sleep.

'Pretty sure. I feel like I've slept for a long time.'

'The alarm hasn't rung yet, has it?'

'No. Should do soon.'

It is the storm that has woken them up, beating the windows with a malicious vigour. Lily gets up and walks to the large window opposite their bed.

'The sky is black,' she says. Not ink-black, but dark enough that it takes a while to make out the shape of rain. It's coming down hard, so hard that there will certainly be trouble. That must be why her heart felt so heavy as she woke, the sound an omen of destruction seeping into her dreams.

'Good, I was getting sun-sick,' Joel says. But it's still so hot that Lily's skin sticks to her like wet clothes.

Now that her eyes are used to the darkness, she can look back towards the bed and see her boyfriend's shape, pale lean limbs stretching out from under the covers. *I don't love him anymore*, she thinks. *I don't know when I stopped.*

'Come back to bed,' Joel says, and she can't bring herself to respond. After a moment, he sighs. 'I see the day's off to a great start. What the fuck is wrong with you?'

Can't you see everything is wrong?

'I hate it when you play mute.'

'We need to get dressed,' Lily says, standing very still by the window. She does not want to get dressed; there is sweat running down her spine, and the humid air weighs down on her. She wants to be submerged in icy water, not enclosed in fabric. The alarm rings, and Joel smashes the button down with too much force. It doesn't break.

'No need to rush,' Joel says. 'Morning like this, everyone's going to be late anyway. Streets must be flooded by now. Malcolm wouldn't even care if we didn't go in.'

'I want to go to work. I have a lot of applications to finish processing.'

'Okay, okay. But, like I said, no need to rush.'

Lily crosses the room to create some distance between them. She flicks the light switch in the corner. Nothing happens.

'It seems there is a blackout.'

'What a fucking surprise,' Joel barks. After last summer's storm surges cut off Sizewell C from the national grid, the absence of light has become a more commonplace experience. With neither nature nor artifice to serve as illuminators, darkness has free rein to swallow the city, adding insult to the injury of sunless July mornings.

'Well, that's another reason to be late,' Joel says, still half under the covers. Lily glances at him to see he's touching himself, moving his hand in a lazy, steady pace. She wishes he would just take care of it himself, but she knows what happens next. Despite the heat, there is a chill going down her body, almost like a cold electric current. *I shouldn't be dreading this*, she thinks. *He's my boyfriend. He has a nice body. I used to love him.* Suddenly Joel is behind her, hands encircling her bare waist. The sensation of his hardness on the small of her back used to make her light-headed, hungry for it, but now she wants nothing more than to push him away.

'What's gotten into you? You're stiff as a board.'

'I don't know,' Lily says. 'Nothing.' *When did I become this weak?* It's not like she's ever had trouble saying no to men before. She's broken a nose or two, for fuck's sake. It's just that she's never had to say no to Joel before. There didn't used to be any reason to practise denial. 'I really don't know what's gotten into me.'

'Maybe we can work it out together,' Joel breathes into her neck, and it only makes everything worse. *Fight or flight?* She has caught glimpses of this feeling before: *do I really want to be doing this? Should I be doing this?* rattling inside her mind all of a sudden while they're having sex, feeling the same frozen chill when he lays his hands on her for the first time in a while. But they have been just flashes, momentary discomforts she has pushed down. His hands still feel good on her, his body fits in a familiar way; sometimes the edges get rougher, and that's good too. This is the first time she has felt so petrified, seizing up and failing to soften herself to his touch again. *It must be because I realised I don't love him*, she reasons. *I allowed myself to feel it and it was like stepping into a frozen pond.* If only it were possible to rewind time, she would come up with something to distract herself, and would never allow herself to go so far down that line of thought. *I can't afford to go through this.*

'If I said no, what would you do to me?' is the big question, the one she hasn't really thought about before. They are both capable of violence. That's what drew them together, after all.

'I'm sorry, I'm feeling a bit strange today. Must be the storm.'

'That's exactly why I said we should stay in bed, see if it passes. Could light up some candles, get a bit cosier.'

She turns around to kiss him, then pulls away to whisper, 'I prefer the darkness, sometimes,' trying for seductive but still sounding sombre. 'I can feel you better.' She glides her fingers down his body. They are both sticky with sweat already. It's awful, having sex in a heatwave, in a storm that has made the whole sky a big black eye looking down on them in hatred. 'Want to see if you can make me feel better?' Going through the motions, it's easy enough to keep the nausea down. Human bodies can adapt to almost anything – their homes being swallowed by the sea, their food and clothes and movements being rationed so carefully, the sharp metallic taste of water from the public collection points, the stench of death past, present and future lingering over everything, the caress of a lover your mind has already finished rejecting.

Afterwards, Lily walks back to the window, a towel draped around her shoulders. They should wash themselves before work, really, but the shower room in the basement seems so far away. The stairwells are dark, the locker room is dark, everything is still dark. Maybe the clouds will break apart at some point; surely this storm must end sometime. Days like this make Lily think of the never-ending rain in *One Hundred Years of Solitude*, how she used to wonder if Márquez was really a time traveller, if the title referred to a century he had crossed to write about things nobody around him could yet know. It was a juvenile thought, but then she'd only been a child at the time it occurred to her, leafing through a paperback that had already been tattered by the time Mia had gifted it to her. It remains the only book of fiction Lily has ever read cover to cover, at least if she counts the parts Mia read to her. They would lie in the narrow bunk bed, curtains closed, setting the scene, Lily holding the small flashlight like a conductor's baton, carefully moving the spotlight down the page as Mia read in her gently hushed voice, taking both of them somewhere beautiful. Now, the way their knees touched outside the circle of light, the way Mia took a small inhalation of breath before embarking on a new paragraph, feels much more a fabrication of memory than the content of the book itself. Lily has heard that every time you reconstruct a scene from the past in your mind it gets a little more distorted, so she tries to think of Mia as little as possible. Sometimes she worries she's already lost her completely.

If this rain would never end, the swollen river would wash this city away once and for all, finally sweeping the banks clean of these overgrown structures that leeched off the soil. The remaining things would all rot; Lily imagines her heart gradually being covered by mould, her lungs being clotted by its slimy residue.

Desert crossing

MIA LEAVES HER little concrete perch overlooking faulty cablings and other broken things, heading past the substation towards a colourless nothing, and gets lost in the storm. It is what she needs to do. She melds into the rain because her body is sixty percent water, because she wants nothing more than to be part of it, not to drown but to fall, fall, fall, endlessly, without intent or responsibility. She keeps walking at the fitful pace of someone without direction or destination. Maybe the wind will suddenly take hold of her and carry her to her proper place. Maybe the rain will lift like a stage curtain and she will be blinded by some kind of a revelation. These are the secret hopes she clings to, stumbling down grey streets and muddy parkways. Her shoes soak up the wetness they tread, sponge-like. Within their damp containers, her toes grind together painfully. With every step there is a squelching sound, and she's not sure if there is blood mixed in with the water. She's too scared to stop, because walking feels like swimming against the current now, except that instead of drowning she would merely collapse. The rain keeps beating on her shoulders, urging her to keep moving.

Of course, there comes a point where the clouds drift apart again, flooding the earth with light. Mia is standing in the middle of a road she does not recognise, surrounded by low houses and grassy fields heaving with the weight of water. It is the moment after some terrible spell has been lifted, and the mundane tranquillity of the ugly suburb is soothing. Having measured the progress of the day only in her muddled footsteps, Mia has lost track of the hours, but the sun is still high. A thin sheet of rain falls through the clear air.

At the end of the quiet road, Mia sees an open gate and limps towards it. It leads her into a large park where straggly trees grow close to the rusted fence. Mia leans against their solid bark to rest for a while and inspect the damage. She squeezes her eyes shut while pulling her shoes and socks off, takes a deep breath and steals a glance at her feet. Nothing red. She sighs.

In the centre of the park she sees a group of people. It is the first gathering she's witnessed during her sojourn through the storm. They are standing in a formation – a queue. Some of them are opening umbrellas, now that the rain is light enough to ward off. Some are wearing shiny raincoats, but most of them are dressed in clothes that must have been raggedy even before they were ravaged by the weather. Mia walks towards them, awkwardly holding her soiled socks and shoes. Two figures are handing large canisters to those who wait from a tiered trolley beside them. One is a young black woman, her hair tied with a long red ribbon, and the other is a blonde white woman with an islander's face, wind-carved and severe.

'Good morning,' the blonde woman calls out.

'Good morning,' Mia says, surprised at how level her voice sounds. She feels wrung-out, wretched, washed up, cleansed.

'You've been walking through the storm to get here?' the woman with the red ribbon asks.

'Yeah. You can tell?' Mia says. The woman chuckles. Her smile is the kind of distraction Mia has almost completely forgotten about.

'How come? You need some drinking water?' She turns away to hand a translucent container to an old man.

'No, no. I didn't actually intend to come here. I mean, I don't know where I am, and I don't know who you are. I just needed to walk. Sorry, this sounds weird.'

'Don't worry, it's none of our business.' The woman hands Mia a piece of bread. 'You look like you should have something to eat.'

Mia wants to refuse – surely this generosity isn't warranted – but recalls she hasn't eaten a single bite since waking up. 'Thank you.'

'Do you have a container on you?'

Mia nods and unstraps a flask from her belt. The woman fills it from a large canister of water.

'What is it that you're doing, if I may ask?'

'Distributing essentials.'

'Oh.'

'What about yourself? What do you do?' she asks, her ribbon shimmering in the weak sunlight.

'I work at the substation up the road – well, I'm not sure where I am exactly. Crayford substation.'

A woman in the queue turns to glower at Mia, a baby strapped around her waist. 'You say you work at the substation?'

'That's correct.'

'Well, why are you here instead of fixing the blackout, looking like you've just crawled out of a swamp? Is the job done already? Didn't look like that half an hour ago.' The baby starts to cry, and Mia cringes at the shrill sound.

'We've got to wait until the storm passes. Until the less affected stations can spare us some power to run the extractors.'

'That sounds ridiculous. Shame on you.'

'Shame on this government,' the woman with the red ribbon chips in.

'I'm not a bureaucrat. I'm not even in the Party,' Mia says.

'What does it say on your uniform?' the woman in the queue asks.

Mia looks down at her chest, as if she doesn't remember. 'Central Grid.'

'That's a government agency. Why are you still working for them?'

'I studied environmental engineering so I could help people,' Mia says, almost robotically. It is a sentence she has repeated in her head endless times since starting her job, and has never had any reason to utter out loud before. She wasn't expecting the words to sound so hollow and unconvincing.

'You've got the highest grades in your year,' her teacher had told her in her final year of college. 'You could get a scholarship to study almost anything you want. But I would like to see you do something useful. Keep working hard, and give back to society for all you've received.' Mia had clung onto those words, even though the weight of them was almost unbearable. She had put away childish dreams of studying history or literature, a decision facilitated by the fact that regional humanities departments had been shut down the year before she finished her exams. Studying something frivolous would've required her to move to London, and she wanted to stay close to home for as long as it was physically possible. Even though she had no family to turn her back on, running away from the city that raised her would have felt like a betrayal.

So Mia stayed and worked hard enough to prove her worth, a constant background noise of bad news keeping her company. As opportunities to apply the technologies she was studying became impossible, one tipping point and funding cut and government failure after another, she kept quiet and worked on her impossible problem sets, cramming through blackouts in flickering candlelight. Last autumn Mia had graduated with a distinction, which was enough to make her employable after the inevitable evacuation. She'd been hoping to work on wave and tidal projects, but nothing of the sort was available. Still, she felt fortunate to receive a placement in a government-affiliated graduate scheme in London without even going through an interview stage. On a bitter January morning, just a few days before the election, she'd packed her belongings into three boxes and boarded the train to London. It was almost too late to leave; it was as early as she could possibly have left.

'And this is the best you can do?' the woman in the queue asks, snapping her back to the uneasy present.

Trying to explain the way she's made sense of her life to anyone else, Mia feels as though she simply chose the path of least resistance over and over again only to interpret her actions in the most high-minded way possible. She doesn't know what else to say, so she repeats other lines that have been ricocheting through her head while doing work that was less fulfilling than she'd expected it to be. 'Access to energy is a human right. I think the fact we are failing to ensure that is obviously wrong, but we don't have the resources we need. It's an accumulation of failures.'

'I suppose you need your excuses for adding to those failures,' the woman says with an eye roll. Absorbing spite has never been one of Mia's strong suits. She wants to defend herself, but hangs her head in shame instead, feeling inadequate in the face of the women handing out supplies.

'Leave it, Nora. It doesn't help to harass ordinary people trying to get by. She said she's not a party member,' the woman with the red ribbon says and turns to Mia. 'What's your name, my love?'

'I'm Mia.'

'Good to meet you. I'm Kadeja, and my comrade here is Alice,' she says, nodding towards the blonde woman. 'Now stand back for a minute, will you please; we've got to finish handing these out. I'd like to have a word with you once we're done – a friendly word – so don't run off just yet.' She bends down to take a parcel of something from a steel box by her feet and hands it to the boy at the front of the queue.

It's been months since Mia really talked to anyone other than Rhys, and she's forgotten how to look at herself through the eyes of someone who isn't him, someone who questions *the way things are done*. It is embarrassing to be seen, especially in this strange emotional state. Mia wanders away from the queue, towards a beautiful sound rising above the drizzle of rain. Beneath a large ash tree, a woman in a baggy yellow raincoat is singing. She is out of place, a spot of sun in a grey world that holds no space for her, and Mia's first instinct is to feel second-hand embarrassment – how can this person make herself be heard so loudly? – but she seems self-contained and completely uninterested in what is happening around her, her eyes closed as she lilts through a lacrimal chorus in a language Mia doesn't understand. After the song comes to an end, the woman opens her eyes and sees Mia standing there, watching. 'Do you like the tune?' she asks.

'It's very sad.'

'Fits a day as miserable as this.'

'What is it about?'

'The same as most of them, unhappy love. Having your soul rejected.'

'Your voice is beautiful.'

'Thank you. Do you sing?'

Mia shakes her head. 'I've never really tried.' Only in rare moments such as this, when she is confronted by music, does she realise its absence from her everyday life. It has not always been like that. She used to spend lunch breaks hiding in the music room, her fingertips pressing down on heavy keys in search of beauty, the gaze of her audience of one burning the nape of her neck as she carved out places somewhere outside their usual space-time continuum. She remembers how powerful it felt; now, it seems impossible to reach that state.

'It's very good for you,' the woman says, and looks like she's about to make some other remark, but is interrupted by Kadeja walking up to them. She greets the singing woman before turning to Mia. 'Poor thing, you're soaking wet. Did you really walk all the way from the substation in that hoodless coat?' At first, Mia thinks she must be mocking her, but her tone is gentle.

'I'm fine.'

'I'll give you a raincoat before we leave. I insist.'

'Thank you.'

'There is something I want to show you,' Kadeja says. 'Follow me.'

'Sure,' Mia says and follows Kadeja towards the fence enclosing the park. It soon becomes clear there is nothing out of the ordinary to observe, just wet grass and patches of mud.

'It's better to talk in private,' Kadeja says. 'My instincts have served me pretty well so far, but I need to spell this out. Don't mention us – the things we do or the things I tell you – to anyone.'

'Why would I do that?'

Kadeja smiles, but her eyes are steely. 'Good girl.'

'I think what you are doing is important.'

'I'm glad you see it that way. A lot of people get a cushy job and pull the ladder right up behind them.'

'Nobody has it that cushy these days.'

'Oh, some people do. Those in power want us to think we're all suffering. Let me tell you, suffering is not an equitably distributed resource.'

'I try not to think about it that much. Politics, I mean. I've never really taken an interest in it – it's all beyond me,' Mia says with an apologetic shrug.

'Well, if you ever want a change of pace, you're very welcome to join us.'

'What does that mean? Are you part of a bigger group?'

'Yes and no. We were inspired by the manifesto of this trans-national organisation called Weather Underwater. But it's very decentralised and we're barely in touch with the other groups. Besides, we haven't had much time to focus on strategy since the election and this whole fiasco with water and other shortages. We have our hands full with basic distribution, and even that is getting harder every week. It's not easy to imagine a path to real power.'

'So it's a political party?'

Kadeja laughs, and it makes Mia's heart sink a little, as though she's failed an important test. 'There is no electoral democracy for people like us, although some people are yet to find that out the hard way. Did you vote in January?'

'No,' Mia says. 'I had nobody to vote for. I tried to just ignore the whole thing.'

'So you do get it,' Kadeja says. 'Would you like to hang out and learn more sometime?'

'I would like to.' Mia is surprised by how certain her answer feels. She can't quite shake the feeling that she is being initiated into some kind of a cult, but the way Kadeja speaks is so sincere.

'Next Saturday, July 2nd, at noon? Meet me by Nunhead Cemetery. North gate – the one in Linden Grove. Do you know how to get there?'

'I will figure it out.'

Kadeja looks at her, softer now, and beautiful in a way that makes Mia feel a little fragile. They walk back towards Alice, who is packing things into the trolley now that the people have dispersed. 'Would you give me the clothes bag, please,' Kadeja says to her.

'I don't think I'll be needing the raincoat,' Mia objects. The clouds are finally splitting, drowsy and half-lidded.

'Take one just in case,' Kadeja says, already shoving one into her arms. 'Some friends of ours found a massive batch of textiles in a warehouse the other week. It had been sitting there for God knows how long. Does this look like twenties' fashion to you?' It is a dark red coat with a plasticky matte surface.

'I couldn't tell. I have no eye for that sort of thing.'

'Try it on for me.'

Mia obliges, and Kadeja beams at her, delighted. 'You look like Little Red Riding Hood. Very cute. Stay away from wolves on your way back.'

Mia thinks Kadeja must be flattering her to make sure she'll show up on the weekend, but it still throws her off balance. 'No, I don't,' she says with a wince. 'But thank you.'

'Take care till Saturday. I'm looking forward to it,' Kadeja says by way of farewell.

Mia walks back to the substation with a more confident step, the red coat folded under her arm. She can see where she's going and picture the tasks ahead. She must. Because if she stopped focusing on them – putting one squelching wet shoe ahead of the other and trying not to wince in pain, making a list of things to do when they finally get reconnected to power – she would fall into the swirling depths of uncertainty, strange songs and strong hands, cold gazes and rushing blood, the long tails of red ribbons twining about her.

Hit

LILY STARES THROUGH the window, watching the dust on the glass form patterns in the grey sky. She is refusing to look at her mother's wide red eyes, instead fixating on the off-white envelope on the table, a line of divide. The social workers have just left. 'You look so ugly when you cry,' Lily says and takes a sip of her already lukewarm tea. She's seen that face enough times to know it without looking. Her mother inhales sharply.

'You can say whatever you like to me,' she says. 'God knows I probably deserve it. But did that boy deserve what you did to him?'

'I don't care.'

'I just wish I could understand.'

'I can't help it if you're stupid.'

'You might be worse than your father.'

They sit in silence for a long time, feeling resentment oscillate in the air in changing directions, ebbs and flows, growing fainter only to return with a vengeance. Her mother covers her eyes with her hands.

'I agree with them, you know. I don't think I can look after you anymore.' She tries searching for Lily's gaze again, fails and sighs in resignation. 'To be honest, I am a little scared of you.'

Lily jolts in anger. 'Why? You know I'd never hurt you.'

'What if you do something even worse the next time? I'm dreading a call saying you've stabbed someone in the throat instead, or been stabbed yourself. You're my little girl, but I feel like I've already lost you.'

'Maybe I'm not your little girl then, and I should go. I'll be glad to be rid of this fucking dump anyway.' This anger is the one thing Lily has to hold on to. The moment her hand twitched at the handle of the knife, the moment she drew blood, it was white hot, blinding. Now it has cooled just so she can see the faint outlines of what lies beneath, and she knows this is the furthest she can go.

'Don't think this is easy for me,', her mother says. 'You've been the one good thing in my life.'

'You can't pin your hopes on me,' Lily spits. 'I don't owe you anything.' She storms out and spends the night in directionless motion, looking at things without really seeing them. At sundown, she stands on a hill and watches the rusted spires of the cathedral jutting out of the sea. She remembers walking in the old town with her mother and her grandma during a festival once, seeing people in fancy costumes selling old-fashioned trinkets. The cathedral towered over them, tall and dusty. Those memories may just as well be false; the people in them are all faceless. Still, she knows the old town was still there when she was small. It was the first one to go, which seemed appropriate, as it had had a pretty good run already. By the time she's twenty, the whole city centre will be submerged. Everyone knows that, but they pretend they don't. Lily is not good at pretending. That's why she can't justify putting on her school uniform and going to class and following all the pointless rules day after day. This cursed city is a wooden ship chewed by maggots, carrying liars and traitors further and further into the open sea, and she can't wait for the day it finally sinks.

Ministry
of Water

'I HAVE TO speak my mind. I am a white British citizen. I started paying tax when the GRS was still called Her Majesty's Revenue and Customs, and haven't stopped since then. Now that my home's gone under, I've been put to live the rest of my days alone in an evacuation centre and, let me tell you, it's like living in a shoebox. Why can't I at least use as much bloody water as I like? Is this quota not a violation of my human rights?'

'I have sympathy for your frustration, sir, but I assure you that the personal quotas have been calculated with care. They are perfectly reasonable and correspond to the most accurate scientific information we have available.'

'What kind of scientific information is that?'

'Nobody here is dying of thirst. Under extraordinary circumstances, such as giving birth at home, a special permit can be applied for.'

'Even if it's a measly amount for some, it's breaking my back, carrying mine and my wife's allocations every day. I'm sick of the sight of these buckets.'

'We do provide an assistance service for transporting – '

'For fifty quid a month! How are we supposed to afford that

with only my pension? We voted for you, believing you'd claw the power back into British hands, and now we're being treated as second-class citizens all the same. It's one betrayal after another.'

'These are simply interim measures to tide us over the current crisis and secure our democracy for the long term. In time, we will be able to provide plentiful clean water and other resources for everyone, most of all pure British citizens.'

'Why're you giving water away for all the scum anyway? Why not just let them dry out in the sun? That should free up resources for the rest of us.'

'I am not in a position to discuss the central government's demographic resource policy. All I can say is that these quotas must be monitored and respected for the time being, in order to ensure our current level of population has its basic needs met.'

'My daughter is a cleaner, and she tells me some houses are still connected to the water mains. She sees people taking hot baths every day, even swimming in their own pools, for God's sake.'

'That is categorically untrue. The same rules apply to everyone, including the Prime Minister, who gets her water deliveries subsidised but nonetheless processed the same way as anybody else's. If you have any practical policy suggestions, please direct them to your MP. I have run out of time to take questions.'

Private person

MIA PEELS HER wet socks and shoes off on the substation steps, sighing in relief. Through the glass door that separates their office and living spaces, she sees Rhys sitting at the dining table, head in the cradle of his palms. The sound of the door makes him drop his hands and look up. Mia realises she's still holding the bundle of red cloth Kadeja gave her and feels a pang of anxiety, but all Rhys says when she enters the room is: 'We're getting connected in twenty minutes.' Mia exhales in relief. It would have been humiliating if her anxious detour had delayed the repairs. She can't decide whether she is more glad or disappointed that Rhys doesn't acknowledge her unexplained absence in any way.

'How much have you had to drink?'

'Not too much to work.' His face is very red, but there would be little benefit in arguing about this.

Mia goes into her claustrophobic room and gets changed into a dry uniform. She sits on the bed and stretches her legs, keeping them suspended in the air until her stomach starts cramping. She closes her eyes and listens to the silence. It sounds like something is ending.

Outside, they run the extractor pump until the broken sealants are above water. The sight makes Mia viscerally angry at whoever failed to do their job. She knows she is a hypocrite, having wandered off while on standby. Still, she is here now, and she will make sure it's fixed for good.

It takes long enough that they need to use headlamps for the final check-ups. They miss the sunset, the storm's radiant afterbirth. Rhys holds up better than Mia expected, despite the barely-there tremor of his fingers. Mia handles the finer details gladly. 'I think it's good to go,' she says. 'Let's run some final tests.'

For a few hours, Mia's hands are busy and her head has no room for anxiety or uncertainty, just the steady hum of thoughts about how to solve the problem staring them in the face. Up to her elbows in a problem that she can solve, she grasps at the full feeling of purposefulness after crossing its pale shadows day after day. It is intoxicating. She catches herself wishing she could feel this way more often, but that would require more storms, more reasons to push the panic buttons. That is another desire to be shoved down and suffocated in the dark.

Once the lights are back on and their work clothes are off, Rhys takes a half-full bottle of gin from the kitchen cupboard. The liquid glimmers yellow in the lamplight, unappetising.

'Did you get too sobered up while working?'

'Shut up. I simply want to make a toast.'

'Why?'

'We just successfully completed a very important job.'

'It's literally just our job.'

'You are no fun.' Rhys pours out an irresponsibly generous serving and hands it to Mia. 'Cheers.'

'Cheers.'

'Now drink up, girlie.'

'Don't call me that.'

Mia fights against the urge to withdraw into her room and just go to sleep. She only resists out of a sense of pity for Rhys, who seems simultaneously all too content with the way things are and steeped deep in malaise. He seems like the kind of man who would be happiest at home with a big family. He is at least a decade older than Mia, technically her supervisor in the graduate programme, and she doesn't really know how he ended up manning this desolately suburban substation on his own. He has probably volunteered that information at some point, but Mia tends to listen to him only in emergencies. They are a terrible match. Rhys pours himself another glass and takes out a deck of cards.

'Black Jack?' he asks.

'Why not?' Mia concedes. After three rounds, they have achieved a perfect symmetry of one win each and one tie.

'You know I'd never come on to you,' Rhys says while shuffling the cards.

'I think I do, but having it spelled out like that is a little unnerving.'

'Do you know why that is?'

Mia takes a sip of her gin instead of responding, so he goes on.

'I think you're a lesbian.'

'What?'

'Am I wrong?'

'It's none of your business.'

'Look, I wouldn't judge you if you were. I just find it weird that we've been working together for months and I've never heard you talk about this stuff. Have you ever even had a boyfriend?'

'I'm just a private person.'

'I guess it's harder to be open about this stuff when you are from an immigrant background.'

'That has nothing to do with this. I wasn't even raised by my parents.' Rhys knows this. Mia has had to explain more than once that she was an orphaned ward of the state at a young age, but he cannot or will not remember.

'Fair enough,' Rhys says, flashing his palms apologetically. For a brief, tense moment, they continue playing in silence.

'So, feel free to ignore my question, if you think it's inappropriate, but I'm really curious. You're, what, twenty or twenty-one? You don't seem to be into boys much. Are you still a virgin?'

'Shut up,' Mia says with as much force as she's mustered all day. 'I'm going to bed.'

'One more round?'

'No.'

'Come on, stay for another drink. I just wish we could get to know each other a little better. Who else do I have to talk to?'

Talk to God, Mia thinks, but she knows better than to poison the air on purpose. She wipes her glass clean and tiptoes back to her room, her ship cabin, her prison cell. The walls are bare, and the one window is barely larger than an envelope. It is the smallest, most depressing room Mia has lived in – she never knew how good she had it in the orphanage and at her university halls. She has never felt very sure about what constitutes a home but, at least in hindsight, there have been times she has almost grasped it – lit-up windows awaiting her at night, the soft dust of time accumulating on every surface, the gauze of continuity coiling around her. She's only halfway through her contract here, but it's already clear that this space will never be more than a waiting room. Mia lies down on top of the bedcovers and closes her eyes, dreams of killing something with her bare hands.

Cleanse

LILY STARES OUT into the remnants of the storm, a towel draped across her shoulders in a weak attempt to soak up the sweat. The electricity hasn't come back on yet, but the sky has lit up in a hazy afterglow of violence. The whole day has felt detached from reality, an indecipherable footnote to life, such as these storm-swallowed days tend to be. Codified by some type of resignation to powerlessness, these are futile hours spent mostly in bed, fucking and trying to sleep, or putting together plates of tinned food. Lily finds she enjoys each of these activities less and less, even if she finds the shaded malice of storm surges preferable to the more urgent desperation of endless sun struck days, where the only place that feels remotely safe is the mortuary chill of the office.

'You're being really quiet today,' Joel says. He's still in bed, propped up against a pillow, straining to read a book in the low light. 'Are you ill?'

'No. I already told you, it's the weather. I'm sick of it.' She turns to look at him. 'Could we walk to work?'

'Are you that desperate to go in? It's already afternoon. I'm sure your permits can wait until tomorrow.'

'What if there's a new storm tomorrow?'

Joel sighs. 'Fine. I'll come with you, if it's so important to you.'

'I thought it was important to you too.'

'Oh, don't doubt my loyalty to the Party. I just think that hours in the office rarely correlate with the amount of things you actually get done.' He taps his temple. 'Most of the work happens here.'

'I can't stamp the documents with the power of my mind. And I'd rather not ruin others' travel plans if I can help it.'

'Quit just standing there then,' Joel scoffs, already putting his boots on. 'Put some clothes on, if you're in such a rush.'

They wade through the streets while the overflowing gutters garble like choked-out animals. The deep puddles reflect the lights of buildings that have their own power generators. In a year or two, Lily hopes they'll be allowed to move into one of those newer, sleeker flats with their own bathrooms with running water and micro-sized fuel cells safely tucked away inside the kitchen cupboards. These new government-allocated housing units are reserved for top civil servants, military personnel and other high-level individuals. Rumour has it that they have been connected directly to the public water lines, but Lily doesn't know if it's true, since she has never visited any of these flats. She knows Joel has some high-level connections – that is why he could get her hired so easily, even despite her past transgressions, or maybe because of them – but he likes keeping his cards close to his chest.

Through the windows all she can see is geometric lamps shining down on dining tables decorated with books and flower vases, brightly coloured sofas populated by neatly dressed people. Sometimes there are children in expensive school uniforms doing their homework, eyebrows scrunched together, and occasionally passers-by are treated to the sight of someone getting railed against a table, the lovers' lit-up silhouettes unmistakable in darker weather. From the street you can see lots of things, but not a peek of anyone filling a bath with running water and luxuriating inside it. Lily imagines herself soaking in a bath with some rose petals thrown in for good measure, her flushed cheeks tingling with the heat from the steaming pink water and from the guilt-tinged glee coursing through her veins. Perhaps one day she'll make it; the possibility is real enough that she can almost smell the flowers and, if she gets that far, surely she can drown her guilt as well.

Their current flat is a relic of the past, built long before summer storms furious enough to debilitate nuclear power stations, before sweltering pitch-dark heatwaves, before the need to ration drinking and bathing water. The vast majority of private bathrooms have simply been cut off from the mains. Although Lily and Joel only have a communal one in the basement, they get their drinking water delivered straight to the door on a government subsidy. Most people carry their allocations in makeshift containers, making a daily journey through crumbling streets and twisting stairwells. To wash, they pour it over themselves inside their defunct baths or shower stalls, or soak tea towels to wipe off the dirt. Lily has heard people on the street talk of smart containers being introduced soon, machines which can calculate the household's water quota and even incorporate a self-driving function to remove the need for manual labour, but she figures it must be wishful thinking to help people take the edge off their anger.

Watching old women drag around steel buckets, backs bent and cracked lips sighing, Lily always thinks of her mother. If she's not long in her grave, she must be crawling the streets to avoid it. Sometimes Lily wonders what would happen if she ran into her mother on the street, but she knows it's never going to happen. Even if her mother were alive, there is no way she would have chosen to evacuate to the capital.

They cross Vauxhall Bridge. Double decker tops and other debris – dead LCD displays, sopping wet clothes snagged on tree branches, half-transparent polystyrene shoals and polypropylene islands mixed with decaying organic matter – peek out through the surface of the water, black like a dense mass of ink this morning. If Lily had grown up around here, she'd probably find the sight of these drowned buses and landmarks heart-breaking.

'What are you thinking of?' she has the impulse to ask Joel as they walk up quiet side streets. The main thoroughfares are badly flooded, the Thames growing multiple additional arms to try and strangle them with.

'Not much.'

'You're always thinking of something.'

'Half-formed thoughts. Wouldn't want to speak carelessly.'

'What does it matter if I know your half-formed thoughts? Don't I deserve to know? I could kill you in your sleep, for God's sake.' Lily intends the words as affectionate, but they come out harsh, hanging between them like a real threat.

'You wouldn't dare,' Joel says, grinning at her. Fortunately for Lily, he is not the type to be easily intimidated.

'Guess you'll have to find out.'

Joel smirks at her. 'I'm looking forward to it. I hope you're at least inventive with the murder weapon. A pillow on the face would be deeply disappointing.' He pinches her a little too hard on her upper arm. 'What are you thinking of, anyway?'

'Baths.'

'A lie is no better than silence.'

'I'm not lying.'

They enter the Ministry of Social Affairs, swiping their chips at the ornate entrance. In government buildings Lily often feels as though she is visiting a museum, or a very large and fanciful time capsule. Most of the time it is a comfort; sometimes it fills her with dread for the world outside. Power generators run silently under their feet. The bright and cool hallways are nearly empty, a handful of people rushing somewhere with manila folders tucked beneath their arms or meandering with a hungry look in their eyes. They make their way to their office, a large open-plan space with desks placed within clean earshot of one another.

'What's the head count today?' Joel asks Malcolm, his second-in-command and a part of the great wave of cops turned civilian after the Ebbtide victory.

'Poole isn't here,' Malcolm says. 'It's already past noon, so I figure he isn't coming in today. It's fair enough, given his commute. You lovebirds, on the other hand, should have walked in hours ago.'

'What's a little tardiness on a day like this?' Joel counters. 'You don't have to fall off a bridge to drown on your way to work.'

'Tardiness, hmm,' Malcolm says, then looks around the room and raises his voice to address everyone present – a bunch of posh white guys with university degrees, neat haircuts and shirts clean enough to reflect the glare of the lamps overhead, and Amelia, the Prime Minister's niece, in possession of what should be an easy desk job. 'Everyone, remember to submit your feedback forms on the deactivation plan by Friday afternoon. I expect most of your opinions to be shit, but in case there are one or two non-shit ideas I'll give you credit for them in the next committee meeting.'

It is unclear what the qualifications required for this line of work are. Lily knows better than anyone in the room, with the possible exception of Amelia, that who you know is everything. She was given this job after Ebbtide won a crushing majority in the January general election, simply by virtue of being Joel's new girlfriend and confidante. Party leadership agreed that Joel had played a reasonably large part in winning the Westminster seat, campaigning tirelessly and, most of all, cleanly. In the run-up to the election several members had been accused of getting their hands too dirty and deflecting from the agenda. The official party line was to never show blood before victory, but some people were too impatient or self-righteous to listen. The worst excesses included a guy in Lewisham who murdered his allegedly socialist neighbour by impaling him with an iron stake covered in carvings of a reversed tsunami wave, the Ebbtide symbol, and carried the severed head to the railway station while shouting words from the campaign manifesto like a raving street preacher; and a young university dropout who wanted to express his support by blowing up a local Jewish primary school. The police found out about the plans, but the protests against his arrest went on for days. All in all, Lily had suspected that these violent incidents did absolutely nothing to quell the popularity of the Ebbtide party. She didn't believe Joel thought so either. Regardless, he had played by the book and been rewarded for it with a stable position in the newly configured party-state machine. By some stroke of luck, Lily was allowed to come along for the ride, and she has held on tight ever since. She understands the gist of it, the central moral code of us versus them. It is a dynamic she is well-acquainted with; even if the boundaries of these groups sometimes seem to shift almost daily, the ideological nuances hardly matter.

After Lily ran away from the foster home at fifteen, she'd spent the remainder of her teenage years floating on and off the street without any life purpose grander than going along with the whims of her friends, a group of losers who had found each other by necessity. The police had labelled them a gang, and they had embraced the term as a badge of honour. They weren't committed to anything, not even violence; they never killed anyone. Sal said he'd stabbed a guy to death at twelve and got away with it, but Lily always suspected it was nonsense. The details of the story kept changing, save for the most crucial one, which was Sal's role as a hero. Sometimes the guy had killed Sal's older brother, other times he was a filthy paedophile preying on the boys' locker room at school and getting what he deserved; in the most outlandish version Sal saved a bunch of girls from being trafficked and got to have sex with each of them as a reward. Nobody ever bothered to press him for further details. Lily herself did stab a boy at twelve, but not to death. That was how she ended up at the foster home at Buckley Street, but it would never have occurred to her to brag about it. She didn't need that false glory. The boys didn't ask her too many questions either; that has always been the good thing about boys.

It was only after Lily came to London that she realised how innocent they had been, even when she'd thought they were anything but. She'd show up with her cuts and her bruises, glowing with the halo of naive perversion, and pull all the real punches. They'd mug rich students on the streets, shoplift from off-licences and indulge in dramatic hostilities with other losers. They rarely ended up in real trouble, until things suddenly escalated the summer before the big wave of evacuations. The boys botched a robbery, one Lily hadn't been told about or allowed to participate in, and ended up in prison. They're as good as ghosts to her, fixtures of a past life. Now that she knows better, she thinks they must have been doomed from the start, running around on borrowed time. Lily's dad had a pit bull when she was very small, and she can faintly remember snuggling her face against its wet nose. It got sick with a brain tumour and spent the last days of its life chasing its own tail, running in circles to escape the unyielding pain generator of its own body.

That image is burnt into Lily's mind. Whatever horrors her mind conjures, she knows she must never fool herself into thinking she can outrun them. Still, she has run pretty far, leaving behind the drowning city with its ghosts.

It has been a year, almost to the day, since she got off the evacuee train in Victoria, dragging her suitcase with its flat wheel behind her through the station square, and heard Joel's voice for the first time. He had been campaigning for a rising political party, reading out a speech in the station square – 'A Promise for A Better Future', as she'd later learn, a piece he'd written a couple of days previously and was very proud of – and it had made Lily stop in her tracks and listen. Truthfully, she had felt overwhelmed the minute she stepped off the train and onto a platform teeming with bare, desperate, blistering life. In her mind, the capital was a site of terror and fantasy. She had dreamed of big city lights since she was a child but, as she grew older, it became clear that this would be where she'd end up when the road ran out. Finding herself in the *now* and *here*, she felt utterly lost. In theory, she knew the procedure: she was to report into the nearest evacuation office, which would start processing her residency application and refer her to a temporary shelter. She was supposed to go on the dole and accept the first shit job they'd offer to a low-skilled, uneducated waste of space like her. She was supposed to start slotting herself neatly back into the proper society she'd sworn off at fifteen. At least she was a full citizen, so she didn't worry about being denied these meagre opportunities. Still, the thought of performing a single one of the required tasks made her feel like she'd swallowed needles. The cold-eyed street preacher had been the first distraction she could find, and it was only natural she threw herself head-first into his world to avoid colliding with the boundaries of her own.

'We need to rise against all whose greed and over-consumption, whose immature impulse for uncontrolled procreation, has flooded our lands and squeezed our soil dry,' Joel had said in his matter-of-fact but captivating tone. At first, Lily had wondered if she was simply easy to impress, but the faces of the crowd around her appeared similarly enthralled. 'They are the reason why our coastal communities are devastated, why we are struggling to quench our thirst with clean water, why we are urged to consider *everything* we used to take for granted an unreachable luxury.' His voice had made Lily recall the mandatory church services of her childhood with its unwavering tone, as though he were exposing truths where everyone else could only grasp in the dark. 'All the Justice Party have managed to do over decades is to keep blaming us, shackling us with the same chains they should use to keep only our enemies down. It's not enough, and we know they'll never go far enough, because they are cowards and race traitors. The Ebbtide party is not afraid to say what we all know is true. We need to reclaim our land and push back the tide by controlling the parasites.'

It hadn't been so much the words but the strange unwavering passion of this man, the way he kept his anger burning at a low flame, that compelled Lily. She had never heard anyone speak like that about worldly things, as though every single word held immense significance. Lily had found herself craving his conviction, and, as it turned out, he was just as drawn to her eagerness. He was drawn to her body too, his hungry eyes and searching hands smoothing down every old scar, the stark angles of her bones over the course of months to come. What made the strongest first impression on him, though, was her temper. As Lily had stood at the edge of the crowd, listening to the speech with her luggage in hand, some unlucky chancer had walked up to her from behind and pressed his body against hers. Joel didn't see the initial contact, a mundane infringement, but he couldn't fail to notice the following altercation.

'What the fuck do you think you're doing?' Lily had snarled, pressing a knife against the man's throat. 'You think I'm just some slab of meat to be grabbed at? Well, you're just the same to me.'

Joel had cut his speech short to break them off before any blood could be drawn. 'Will you come with me?' he'd said to Lily under his breath. 'Let's go before anyone else gets involved.'

'Stranger danger,' Lily had grinned, before following. In hindsight, she wasn't quite sure why she had agreed so easily. Perhaps she was simply trying to make her life someone else's problem.

While it was her sharp edges that initially attracted him, Joel said it was difficult to believe she had spent years on and off the streets because she seemed so *clean*. He liked her skin, her hair, her scent. Lily wasn't used to the compliments, but it was easy enough to just take them, to take everything that was on offer. Of course, it was always intended as a mutually beneficial arrangement. Joel wanted her to help out with the campaigning, which she did – she wasn't expected to say much, just stand under the January rains and winds and give out flyers with slogans printed in deep green and marine blue, words like 'Stop population replacement – remedy the mistakes of the past!' and 'Push back the tide – we are drowning to satisfy parasites!' He bestowed her with a mission and, if she failed to heed that call, then she would deserve to die in whatever ditch she'd inevitably end up at. For someone with no education, no family money, very little charisma or conviction, it is always do or die – make yourself useful to someone, or get kicked to the curb.

Maybe things have changed around too fast, and her head is still spinning, failing to catch up with everything. Falling in love with Joel had been her golden ticket out of the stagnant puddle she was stuck in, her shortcut to a better life. During those last couple of years in Portsmouth she'd known things could not stay the way they were for much longer – even if the sea weren't calling out a doomsday lullaby, promising to pull them all under-water *any day now*, she would've had to leave. With every passing year she'd been sinking deeper into aimless anxiety, getting into mindless fights and seeking pain as a salve for numbness. In the back of her head she knew that what she really craved was a sense of purpose. In that sense, she wasn't different from anybody else. But the longer she spent walking down dead ends, grasping at the loose ends of her youth, the less useful she appeared to important people, the ones hurrying into their classes and meetings in nice clothes, and the less likely they were to ever include her amongst their ranks. Those people had stopped meeting her eyes while rushing past a long time ago. Lily did her best to convince herself that she didn't need anyone else to hold her hand and set her upon a path, that she could find her own way, that she wasn't sinking and, even if she had been, it was her own will to do so; but the truth was she had begun to feel irredeemably lost and more than a little scared, and Joel found her at exactly the right time.

Meeting him had felt like a prescription of revelations running through her veins.

Now she walks through corridors of marble as though she belongs here, and the people around her work hard to uphold the illusion. She sits at a desk by the back wall with her name on it, next to Amelia's. Amelia is poring over a report in silence, her big blue eyes glazed as though she cannot comprehend what she's reading.

'Wake up, Amelia,' Malcolm shouts from across the room, giving her a jolt.

'I wasn't sleeping. I was just trying to understand why this person's permit was denied the last time even though they –'

'You don't need to understand what happened the last time. Just focus on the present. If their permit wasn't granted last time, that's probably a sign that it shouldn't be granted this time either.'

'I just think it would be good to –'

'Don't overthink it.'

Lily takes off her coat and carefully drapes it over the back of her chair. The stack of paper on her desk looms even taller than usual. She needs to make some headway into this or it'll be time for another all-nighter. Her coffee quota is already running low and she knows nobody will let her use theirs – the system turns everyone into a hoarder – except for Amelia, who would bend over backwards for any small request. If Lily ever stooped low enough to ask Amelia for a favour, she would feel unbearably perverse. She sighs and forces herself to focus on the words in front of her.

Request for internal travel (family reasons)
Name: Helen Rhodes.
Age: 52.
Occupation: Nurse.
Ethno-nationality: British (white, non EU).
Postcode: DA5.
Requests permission to travel to: Inverness.
Reasons: Attending daughter's wedding.
Requested means of travel: Train (internal border crossing, 500+ mi).

This woman smiles shyly in the blurry passport photograph glued to the page, her eyes crinkling like half-moons. She seems to be wearing her work uniform, a blue cotton shirt buttoned up to her neck. Lily checks the woman's files on record. She travelled to Inverness and back last July too, a distance of over 1200 miles. For internal travel for family reasons, the annual cap has currently been set at 1000 miles. Lily makes a quick calculation in her head: this woman is white, and a nurse, and wants to travel to her own daughter's wedding. Even if she's not technically allowed to go, Malcom probably won't flag it. She stamps in *Approved* and hopes for the best, closing her eyes in a brief pseudo-prayer before drawing out the next application in the stack.

Reading for long periods of time always makes her eyes hurt. She never imagined herself working in a job like this, filing away documents like a good little secretary. She's probably the last person who should be evaluating all these words, although Malcolm must be even worse.

> *Request for external travel (family reasons)*
> *Name: Ewoka Reid.*
> *Age: 36.*
> *Occupation: Agricultural Production Engineer.*
> *Ethno-nationality: British (Black).*
> *Postcode: SW10.*
> *Requests permission to travel to: Catalonia.*
> *Reasons: Friend's funeral.*
> *Requested means of travel: Flight (external border crossing, 2000+ mi).*

This woman isn't smiling in her official photo. Lily checks her files: no travel during the last year, scholarship-based university degree, flawless tax record. There is nothing to disqualify her, but Lily has a gut feeling she will never get to board her plane. Even though the Party is officially opposed only to immigration, particularly the waves of incoming refugees from other flood-ravaged lands, it is evident that their hostility does not solely apply to newcomers. 'You should always be extra careful when evaluating the applications of non-whites,' a senior Party adviser had told them during their training for this job. 'They are inclined to falsify and omit stuff, to ask for things they *feel* they deserve. You've got to be rational about these things.' Joel and Malcolm might well accuse her of fabricating her engineering qualifications or hacking her chip to wipe records of past travels. Or they might play nice for a bit, following the written-down regulations. That's something Lily has learned over these months on the job. They are always told to follow the operational logic of the big black rulebook but, at the end of the day, it all comes down to the mood of the day. She sticks to the rules and stamps in *Approved*. The boys can take it off the pile later, if they're feeling uncharitable. Lily would never claim political strategy as one of her strong suits, but if she stops and thinks about it, the long-term implications of their favouritism seem damning. When wealthy Party voters with the wrong kind of background start coming out of the woodworks and complaining about having their honeymoon plans ruined by discrimination or bureaucratic incompetence, what is going to be their line of defence? Simply expanding the official categories of undesirables? Then again, Lily wouldn't be surprised if the wealthy simply bribed their way out of the whole permit process. To date, she has not spotted anyone of renown in her heaving stacks of paper.

'Hi, Lily.' A soft whisper interrupts her train of thought. Amelia is standing by her desk, her face crumpled like a sheet of paper someone started squeezing into a ball but didn't quite finish. 'Could I make you some tea?'

'Of course. That's very kind of you.' Lily doesn't dare ask about coffee.

'It's just dandelion. I hope that's okay.'

'It's bitter enough to wake me up.'

Amelia glances at the moat of papers ringing Lily's desk. 'I'll bring it right over for you.'

'Cheers.'

The more Lily sees of Amelia, the more she thinks of her as an office puppy: so adorable that nobody – save for Malcolm – would possibly want to kick her when she's already down, but perpetually in the wrong place, playing catch-up over things that are self-evident to everyone else. A girl with sad limpid eyes and a parentage like hers would solicit love wherever she went. To Lily, the mystery is just how much of it is inspired by her ancestry. Most people see her as a proxy of the Prime Minister, and therefore someone to be wary of upsetting. Only Malcolm doesn't think twice about barking abuse at her. He believes she would never put a bad word in, which appears to be correct.

Lily sees the way Amelia looks at him when she thinks she's being discreet, all softness and longing, as though she had already decided that there must be violence between them, as though she were begging him to do something for her to forgive in silence. Girls like that are a paradox, perpetuating their own victimhood day in, day out, collecting bruises and subcutaneous love-scars like badges of feminine honour. It is an entirely different game from the one Lily tends to play, although the end goal is much the same. Soft girls are alchemists, somehow turning their pain into nourishment, but Lily thinks they are nourishing all the wrong parts, the catalysts of unhappiness. Amelia looks so deeply miserable, always on or beyond the verge of tears. Lily would not be surprised if she and Malcolm were fucking after hours. She meditates on that while waiting for her disgusting tea, resentfully hot in the face.

A couple of hours pass in silence. Lily has only finished about a third of her stack, but her eyes strain and her brain seems to be knocking against her forehead, so she gets up and walks to the staff canteen for her warm meal of the day. It's late enough in the afternoon that nobody else is in, and she relishes the feeling of not being watched.

When she walks back into the office, her guard goes right back up. Joel and Malcolm are huddled over some document on Malcolm's desk, talking in irate whispers. Lily walks past them, careful not to glance at the source of their argument, returning to her own desk to keep working. She can't help trying to listen in, but none of the words are clear enough. Joel leaves the office and returns a few minutes later, a strange expression on his face.

'They agree,' he says to Malcolm in a normal speaking voice and walks over to Lily's desk. 'We have a regulatory meeting to attend this evening,' he says. 'Five o'clock. I'll come fetch you from here.'

'Have I done something wrong?'

'Why would you think that? No, no. Don't worry about it.'

Lily is not sure why, but her body is convinced that this is something to be worried about. A mass of raw anxiety fills her head like a viscous cloud, and she barely gets anything done for the rest of the afternoon. After the courier comes at four, her stack is higher than it was in the morning. She gives up and sneaks into the office kitchen to pour herself a glass of gin.

Strength

IT IS THE coldest night of the year, at least in the dormitory, where the heating is broken and wind rattles the windows like rows of chattering teeth. Mia is hugging her knees under her duvet, trying to will herself into sleep.

'It is easier to fall asleep when in cool temperatures,' Ms. Davis had said before turning the lights off. 'Just stay under the covers and you'll be fine. They're coming to look at the boiler tomorrow morning.'

The hair on Mia's skin is standing up, and it's not just because of the cold. Her body is stuck in a state of anticipation. Maybe she does wade halfway into sleep, but she stays close enough to the surface to be pulled back lightly when the touch on her arm does come. Lily is standing on the ladder of Mia's bunk bed, sticking her hand through the curtain. Her nose and cheeks are bright red, and there is a wild smile on her face. She must have climbed in through the window again. She keeps silent, but her mouth makes the shape of a single word: 'Come.'

Mia is quick on her feet, following Lily down the ladder. All the other girls are breathing in heavy dreams as the two of them slip into the dark corridor. Once they're through the door, Lily takes off her big coat to drape it over Mia's thin nightgown. Mia sees she's still in her school uniform.

'Where have you been all evening?' she whispers. Lily shakes her head and smiles mischievously. 'Check the left pocket,' she says, and Mia pulls out a near-empty glass bottle.

'You've been drinking by yourself?'

'Not by myself.'

'Why didn't you invite me?'

'You wouldn't have come. You're no fun.'

Mia pouts. 'You could have asked anyway.'

Lily puts on an excessively serious face. 'I'm sorry. Did you have a good evening?'

'It was normal. I didn't get into any trouble.'

'You did your homework?'

'Of course.'

Lily grins. 'Good girl. Now, come on. I want to show you something.' She extends her hand and, in the streak of moonlight, Mia sees a band of bruises wrapping around her wrist. She lets herself be taken down, all along the corridor, where the windows let in freezing air like ghost breath. Lily comes to a halt by the door of a storage room. She reaches into the pocket of her coat again, lingering over Mia's body long enough to make her heart skip a beat, and pulls out a ring of silver keys. She opens the door and says, 'After you.' Mia steps into the deeper darkness and waits for Lily to close the door behind her before flicking the light switch.

'Where did you steal the key from?'

'Found it.'

There's that outsized smile on Lily's face again, never wavering as she takes three steps towards Mia, enough to bring them shoulder to shoulder in the small space. The burn of alcohol still lingers on Lily's lips, strong enough to make Mia wonder if it'll intoxicate her too. She's never been drunk before. Still, she knows it's not the alcohol that's making her feel light-headed when Lily's mouth is on hers, so soft, and Lily's hand slots into the curve in her back. Suddenly, Lily grabs the back of her head and bites her lip hard enough to draw out a tang of blood. Mia hisses and pulls back.

'Sorry,' Lily says, lifting her hand over her mouth to emphasise the apology.

'It's okay,' Mia says. 'I just wish you'd be more careful.'

'You really don't like that at all?' Lily sounds a little wounded, staring at Mia as though she's trying her hardest to decode clues hidden in her face.

'What do you mean?'

Lily sighs and lets herself fold onto a pile of spare mattresses in the corner. 'The question is not that complicated.' She has posed it before, with or without words – jagged edges where Mia is expecting softness, tensions building up when she wants nothing but to yield. Sometimes it seems that Lily only knows how to hold things with a white-knuckled grip.

'I'm sorry. I still don't really get it.' Mia feels a sinking feeling in her stomach, as though Lily has suddenly gone somewhere very far away. She sits down beside her on the mattress and interlaces their fingers. 'Where did you get these bruises?'

'Just a fight. A couple of days ago.'

'It must've hurt.'

'Not really.'

'Did you enjoy it?'

Lily scoffs as though the question is completely ridiculous. Mia knows better than to ask too many questions. Instead, she bends down to kiss the bruises on Lily's wrist. 'I hope they'll heal soon.'

Dusting
bluebells

ON SATURDAY, MIA wakes up to the kind of bright blue dawn that could only follow a storm, a brief absolution. It is much earlier than the time she usually gets up, but her excitement keeps her from falling back asleep. She gets dressed more carefully and quietly than she really needs to – it's not like Rhys is going to care or even wake up in time to see her. There is still a small thrill in doing something that feels illicit. Besides, for all she knows, she might be engaging in something actually dangerous. She has moved on from dreaming up occult crucifixions on a moss-covered cross to wondering if the people she met in the park are plotting to kidnap a public agency employee for extortion. She shakes her head at the thought; the way she came across the group was serendipitous enough to be completely innocuous. Besides, she is not important enough to be targeted for something like that. Surely there are higher-up employees, actual governmental employees, who would be easy enough to coax into intoxication and poor decisions. Mia has only been around Ebbtide members during the briefing she received in the beginning of her graduate programme but, from the little she has seen, a high level of intelligence does not seem to be a requirement for joining the Party.

Mia walks into the kitchen to make herself a flask of tea for the journey. Just as the water has started boiling on the stove, a high-pitched buzz cuts through the sound of water. She turns around and sees two men standing on the other side of the glass doors. Neither of them look familiar. She kills the flame and rushes to greet them, her heart in her throat. They never get any visitors here, so why do they have some now, today of all days?

'Good morning,' she says with forced cheer.

'Morning,' the men say. Mia notices the green Ebbtide patches on their jackets.

'Come in, please. I was just making some tea. Would you like to have some?'

'Ah, we're all right for tea. We would just like to sit down and have a little conversation.'

Mia nods. 'You can sit at the table here. I will be with you in a minute.' She goes back into the kitchen to stuff her flask with two teabags and a rush of water, hoping the men won't stay for long.

'Where is your colleague?' one of the men asks.

'He must still be asleep. I could go wake him up,' she offers.

The men look at each other in silent conversation. One of them concludes aloud: 'Well, it's a Saturday. I think we can let him sleep a little longer. He's already been given a preliminary briefing on the assignment.'

'What's the assignment?' Mia asks, sitting down opposite the men.

'We're here to discuss the next steps in the commons deactivation plan.'

'I don't think I've heard of that.'

'You must have heard of the concept.'

'Which is?'

'By the end of the year, we are aiming to turn off all usage of ecosystem services and other infrastructural privileges for those who do not belong in the category of pure British citizens.'

Mia stares at the men. 'Would that include me?'

Both of them laugh. 'How could it? You work for us.'

'But my parents were refugees.'

'Don't you worry, sweetheart. There will be exemptions, including yourself. That is what we're here to talk about. We will provide you with detailed information, and you need to take certain households off the grid in these postcode areas after verifying these – ' they start unfolding a detailed street map.

'Please excuse me.'

Mia stands up and walks out of the glass doors. Her hand is burning: it grips the flask. She walks by the distribution panel board and goes through the motions of morning inspections without writing anything down, turns and rushes down the hill towards the bus stop. She waits for the bus long enough to know the men are not following her, and her chip works on the reader without incident. She knows she's unimportant, replaceable enough, and wonders if they'll at least expect her to come crawling back. She takes a seat behind the driver. The back of his head looks like how she has imagined her own father's looked, the spume of long years riding on waves of black hair. Mia wonders if the driver is lonely, if there is anyone waiting for him. She imagines him finishing his shift, picking up some rations and ascending the stairs to a drab little flat. Flicking the light switch only to remain in the dark. Gazing at rows of yellow squares through his window.

She arrives at the meeting spot Kadeja suggested two hours before noon. The cemetery gates, burning with upside-down stucco flames, are bolted shut, and a carpet of wildflowers spills through the gaps in the fence. Mia wishes she could walk amongst the gravestones, but the fence is too high to climb. Instead, she leans on it and closes her eyes. Those men said Rhys had already been briefed. It fills Mia with disgust, knowing that her colleague has been in on that cruel joke for days or maybe weeks, and how absurd, to think that it's not a joke at all, that they should be working overtime to condemn others to darkness and drought. When she got this position, she had felt like her feet were firmly on the ground of this new and frightful city. Now that has all washed away. All that remains is the uncertain promise of *something* dangled by Kadeja.

She feels like her body will snap with tension unless she keeps moving, so she walks the perimeter of the cemetery. A path of gravel and broken glass twists around the extensive grounds, shaded by solemn trees. It is the kind of path girls are taught never to take on their own. Even in daytime, the shadows fall so darkly it could as well be night. The quality of silence is different, so close to the graveyard. There are whispers just out of reach. Raindrops fall on her face, followed by rays of sun. Fragments of a nursery rhyme float to her from far away.

In and out the dusty bluebells,
In and out the dusty bluebells
Who will be my master?

Who taught her that song? She settles on her mother, although it doesn't make any sense. She doesn't remember her mother's face, let alone her voice.

Mia turns the corner, and Kadeja is standing in front of the gates, waiting for her.

'You came,' Kadeja calls out. 'I'm glad. I wasn't sure if you were really that interested,' she says, but does not look at all surprised to see Mia.

'Thank you for inviting me. Of course I was interested. I was a little worried that it would be difficult for me to leave my post, but going ended up being easier than staying.' Mia glances towards the cemetery. 'The cemetery looks beautiful. I wish the gates weren't shut. I had some time to kill, but I just walked the perimeter instead.'

It takes her aback how easy it is to talk to Kadeja right away. After so many strained silences and forced exchanges with Rhys, to say nothing of the conversation with the visitors this morning, speaking to someone different – someone more like her – makes her feel lighter, every word a little weight off her chest. Besides, there is something about Kadeja that invites openness – an understanding smile, a self-possessed warmth, qualities Mia herself is painfully aware she lacks.

'Some of my relatives are buried there,' Kadeja says matter-of-factly, as though she were equally convinced that Mia is someone to be trusted with personal matters. It is a little embarrassing how delightful it feels to hold such a small piece of information, even a sorrowful one.

'Have you been in?' Mia asks, a slightly obvious question to test the waters.

'Yeah, lots of times. They only closed it in January, to stop people from sleeping there. It's nonsense, really. Who would want to live in a cemetery? I mean, it's an imaginary problem,' Kadeja says, her cadence quickening towards the end. Mia can see that her rage is metallic and brilliant. 'Come on, let's go,' she says, already in motion.

'People must be angry about being barred from the cemetery,' Mia says, struggling to keep up with Kadeja's pace as they walk down the street.

'I know I am. My grandmother's grave shouldn't be without

flowers. I'm sure I'm not the only one who feels this way, but it's not so easy to kick up a fuss these days. At least she was lucky enough to die before the worst of this insanity.'

'I suppose you can see that as a silver lining,' Mia says and cringes at how flat the sentiment sounds. She just doesn't know what else to say.

Kadeja grins at her. 'I like you. You're very serious.'

Mia always gets flustered when others describe her in words. It makes her feel captive – *this is it, these are your outlines. Do you like them?* 'I've been told I'm a bit shy.'

'You have to be told that?'

'It's hard to see yourself.'

'I know, sorry. I was just teasing.'

'Most of the time, I feel like I'm looking at myself from the outside,' Mia explains aloud for the first time. 'I'm never sure if I belong to myself. Even my name – sometimes hearing it makes me feel confused, like calling it forces me into reality. Sorry, this sounds insane.' In this new place, unmoored from memories, she feels even more out of place than usual.

'Don't worry. I think I get it.'

'I've thought about changing my name, but I don't think that would resolve the issue.'

'Probably not.' Kadeja looks at her with warmth in her eyes. 'Besides, I think Mia is a very pretty name.'

'I don't think it's an ugly name. I just wish I knew the name my parents gave me.'

'You don't know it?'

Mia shakes her head. She doesn't usually talk about this kind of thing – it's awkward and it makes her feel doomed, marked for exclusion – but the complex system of self-restraint she has con-structed is short-circuiting.

'My name was given to me by someone in a foster home. My parents tried to come to the UK by sea when I was very small. I suppose our home had washed away, but I don't know where we came from. There were no documents, nothing left, except me.'

'I'm so sorry to hear that,' Kadeja says, slowing down as though she thinks Mia needs a break, or a hug.

'I'm sorry. It's always so awkward to talk about it.'

'No, please don't apologise.'

'Anyway, I know choosing a new name would not make me any happier. The real fantasy is somehow unearthing my true name, and I know that will never happen.'

They turn the corner to Nunhead Lane and walk past rows upon rows of pretty houses. Many of the windows are covered in Ebbtide posters, bold green and blue typefaces spelling out slogans:

LET'S REIN IN THE WAVE OF PARASITES.
STOMP OUT THE LEECHES.

'Did you grow up around here?' Mia asks.

'Yeah, not that far from here. My parents still live nearby, but I don't see them. It's all changed a lot since my childhood.'

'I could say the same about where I grew up,' Mia says with a wry smile.

'Where's that?'

'Portsmouth.'

'Ah,' Kadeja says. 'I thought you might be an evacuee. You don't seem like a city girl.'

'Well, it used to be a city.'

'Not like London is. Was.'

Kadeja stops in front of a large, ramshackle house with boarded-up windows. 'This is home,' she says, fishing a bunch of keys from the bottom of her bag. Mia follows her up the front steps and into the house. It looks abandoned from the outside, but the rooms are full of life: there are mattresses laid out on old hardwood floors, colourful strips of silk hanging from high ceilings, the tail ends of conversations drifting in the air, footsteps above and beneath. It feels warm. Alice, Kadeja's work partner from the park, emerges from a doorway, accompanied by a red-haired young man in paint-stained dungarees.

'You came,' Alice says, looking a lot less stern than the first time Mia met her. Mia nods shyly. 'Welcome. This is my house – on paper, anyway. We all share it now. Kadeja, would you give her a tour?'

'Of course.'

Kadeja introduces the dungaree-wearing boy as Jamie and shepherds the three of them up to an attic room. They cross a large living room with several mattresses laid out on the floor. The wall-length windows are covered in blackout curtains, sucking in the space, and almost every inch of the room is covered in clothes or clutter. 'It's gotten so crowded these days,' Kadeja says apologetically, as though it was her fault that the house only has a finite amount of square metres, or that these people can't find shelter elsewhere.

There seem to be at least three families living in the space. A child waves at Mia, and she returns the gesture awkwardly before disappearing up a ladder. After spending so long in the quasi-wilderness of the substation, integral to the city yet removed from its daily rhythms, Mia feels like a recently incarnated ghost slowly settling into her new flesh. The attic room is dim, despite a small skylight in the ceiling, and two more mattresses are laid out on the floor. The whole house seems like one big bedroom with revolving doors. It reminds Mia of her own childhood.

'This is where we sleep,' Kadeja says, sitting cross-legged on a turquoise pillow. 'Me and Jamie.'

'Are you together?' Mia asks almost unwittingly. The question makes them laugh.

'I'm not into girls,' Jamie says. 'Whereas she is.'

'Oh.'

'What about you?' he asks, flippant, like the words have no weight at all.

'What about me?' she parrots childishly. All her life, she has been trying to exist as unremarkably as she possibly can, constructing a shell to deflect light and attention. Her life might not always have been *easy*, but she is fully aware of her good fortunes, being accepted and supported despite, despite, despite: her skin, her dead parents, her empty child-hands. She'd been the only one in their vessel to make it to solid ground, which could mean she is blessed – that's what a nun visiting Buckley Street once said, cursing the rest of her family in their watery graves – yet she never stopped feeling like she's on thin ice. Even reaching out to Lily, so long ago, she never dared name whatever it was that happened between them. The way their limbs fell together for the first time had felt like a fever dream, a sudden explosion of colours that did not exist in her reality. Whenever Lily opened her mouth and Mia felt a warning tug in her belly, a premonition of unbearable language, she quieted her with a kiss. After Lily disappeared, nothing had threatened her silence for years. She never thought she'd bury her desire forever, but the more time goes by, the less she notices its absence. Its grave is unmarked within a labyrinth of other things that are part of her but only in a pale shadow form.

She is painfully aware that everyone is expecting her to fill the gap in the conversation. What's the worst that could happen here? The faces surrounding her look so understanding.

'I'm not sure,' she says, and immediately feels the answer is lacking.

'Don't put her on the spot,' Kadeja says.

'Sorry. I didn't realise it'd be awkward.' Jamie rubs the back of his neck apologetically.

Kadeja clears her throat and mercifully changes the subject. 'So, Mia. What do you know about us?'

'Nothing, except what you told me,' Mia says, truthfully. 'I just happened to see you giving away water and things in the park and I thought maybe this is something I should be involved in.'

'So you'd never heard of Weather Underwater before?'

'I think I heard something about the assassination attempt on Prime Minister Bain.'

'That wasn't us,' Kadeja rushes to say. 'We don't even know who did it, but it got tagged on us. Naturally. We blew up before the last election, in good ways and bad. We got some new members, including myself, and a lot of fascists were very angry at us. The government has designated us as a terrorist group.'

'Why?'

Kadeja sighs. 'Because we believe it's not up to them to decide who gets to stay in the lifeboat, to borrow their own crude analogy.'

'So you're just trying to help people?'

'That's the most important thing. Of course, we have bigger objectives. Ideally, we'd like to raze this government to the ground and establish a more humane system of governance. But our hands are tied by the lack of resources and' – Kadeja makes an exaggerated hand gesture – '*everything*. Even if our ideas are dangerous to the government, we are in no position to follow through just yet.'

'So, Mia,' Jamie chips in. 'What are you good at?'

'I went to university to study environmental engineering. I don't know anything about governance.'

Jamie flashes a smile at her. 'Oh, good. We don't have many scientists.'

'It's been a slow summer for recruitment,' Kadeja says. 'When we met, you said you work for the central grid.'

'Yeah,' Mia begins. 'Used to, until this morning, at least.'

'Did they sack you for being brown or something?' Jamie asks. Mia notices Kadeja elbowing him in the ribs.

'No' Mia says. 'I left of my own volition this morning. I'm not sure if I'm ever going back. Two Party members came to visit. They told me I should prepare for switching some residents off the grid, based on whether or not they are "pure citizens". I just got up and left.'

'Do you know when?' Kadeja asks.

'No. They were just starting to brief me. Maybe I should've listened to them.'

'It's fine, you're not our informant,' Jamie says. 'I'm glad you got out of there.'

'How long did you work for them?' Kadeja asks.

'About half a year. I graduated and got the job right away. I thought it would be helpful.'

'And now they're requesting your complicity in murder,' Kadeja says.

'Would you really go that far?' Mia asks, slightly defensive. She can picture a version of herself that stayed and followed orders. It is so effortless to imagine the things she could do, vivid because they would be nothing but an extension of the routine she has already completed a thousand times over: washing her face in the greenish light of the control room toilets, pouring water from a canister to a kettle and boiling tea, inspection after inspection, reading old books by lamplight, playing cards with Rhys and feeling the threat of drunken advances hanging in the air between them. She doesn't want any of it, but it has become part of her, and she hasn't fully expelled it yet.

'People will die,' Kadeja says. 'No question about it. Whenever there is a hostile change in policy, it's someone's bullet to bite. You were going to feed it to them.' She places her hand on Mia's shoulder and adds, softer: 'I'm not blaming you for anything. You're here now.'

Mia feels tears brimming in her eyes, and her hands leap to cover her face. How mortifying, to cry in front of strangers. Still, Kadeja's hand feels like an anchor.

Exonerator

'WHY DO YOU never say anything?'

'Because she's a mute.'

'What's a mute?'

'Someone who's too stupid to form words.'

The boys are trying to catch Mia's eyes, but she refuses to return any of their gazes.

'Is she blind as well?'

'No. She's just being weird.'

'Dirty sea slug.'

One of them slams her shoulder against the wall.

'Don't you want me to stop?'

She nods.

'Why don't you tell me to, then?'

He shoves Mia again, harder.

The classroom door flies open, and suddenly Lily is there, squeezing a bright yellow bottle in her hand. The afternoon light is in her hair, and she's standing tall and arrow-straight. 'I'll throw this in all of your faces and make you blind if you don't leave her alone.'

'Fuck off, you crazy bitch.'

'Don't you think being blind would be worse than being a mute?'

Lily starts screwing the cap open, and the boys shriek and scatter. She laughs in that deep unashamed way that Mia envies, and puts the bottle down on a desk with a loud thump. Then she cradles Mia in her wiry arms, squeezing so tight Mia almost forgets where she ends and the world begins. She breathes in the metal smell of chemicals mixed in with Lily's sweet warmth and murmurs into her shirt: 'Where did you get that stuff from?'

'Cleaning cupboard.'

'Would you really have done it?'

'Only if they hit you really hard.' There is a steely glimmer in Lily's eyes. 'They'd deserve to die for hurting you.'

'It's scary when you talk like that.'

'I'm sorry. I won't do it again.'

Lily looks at Mia and cocks her eyebrow. *But you are going to let them bully you again, aren't you?* She might think it all she wants, and it's true, both of them know that. The vicious cycle of her torment perpetuates itself in her stillness, her loss of words whenever they really count. Still, she knows Lily would never say any of it out loud, unlike all the adults around her. She knows it's not that easy. Lily makes everything seem easy but she understands it's really fucking difficult. It's a strength Mia has always lacked, and no matter how close she gets to Lily she'll never be able to absorb it.

Blossom

AFTER HOURS, LILY finds herself staring at a bright blue door at the end of a quiet cul-de-sac. A child's drawing has been taped onto it, ghosts with angry faces and a speech bubble saying 'No junk mail or we will bite!' Malcolm and Joel are standing behind Lily on the front steps.

'What are you waiting for?' Malcolm says as Lily hesitates, her eyes glazing over the little ghosts. The words travel to her hand, which flicks the metal knocker against the door. There's a child's high voice calling from the other side: 'I'll get it!' In a couple of seconds her face appears in the doorway, a happy smile and bright big eyes.

'Hi there,' Lily says, forcing herself to smile. 'Is your mum home?'

'Yes,' the child says.

'Is anyone else home?'

The child raises a finger to her lips, a thinking gesture, as though the question has confused her on some profound level. 'Anyone else?'

'Who is it?' a woman's voice calls out from inside the house.

'Some lady,' the child calls back. 'And two men.'

'Just a minute.'

A woman walks down the hallway in long strides, and the child goes to hide behind her, holding on to the waist of her plain linen dress. There is a strange look of resignation on the woman's face, as though she already knows who they are, as though she has been expecting them. She looks thinner than she should be, her thighs hollowing out in a concave cut to the knee bone, the skin on her cheeks a barely-there veil over her skull. Sometimes you can tell people have been made smaller than their true form, becoming half-shadows either by illness, accident, or design.

'Good evening,' Lily says, an alien smile still frozen on her face. She remembers seeing a photograph of this woman on an application she processed earlier in the day, but cannot recall her name, nor any of her details.

The woman eyes her up and down. 'Good evening. I don't think we've met.' Then her eyes catch Joel's face, and Malcolm's, and widen just slightly. 'Oh, I should've known.'

'I am flattered to hear you haven't forgotten us, Marta,' Malcolm says.

'I've withdrawn from everything that has to do with political activism. You've already won, so what do you want from me?'

'You reminded us of your existence, and we wanted to see your face again,' Malcolm says. He and Joel ascend the remaining steps to stand on Lily's left and right, crowding the entryway in a wordless threat. It should not come as a surprise; she knows well that neither of the men by her side are afraid of using force to get their way. Still, she can't help inhaling some of the acrid fear hanging in the air, letting it contaminate her lungs. Lily has only been told that the objective of this 'visit' is to determine whether or not this woman, with her questionable ethnic origin and her past of illicit activities, is planning to exit and re-enter the country for political purposes, possibly even espionage. She has not been briefed on the methodology of this assessment, but she has her suspicions.

Marta takes a deep breath. 'Is this about my application for a travel permit?' The edge in her voice tells Lily that she is ready to fight. Lily wishes she would just resign herself to her fate and prevent this from getting uglier; but as soon as the wish crystallises, it is tarnished by her awareness that she doesn't even know what fate her colleagues, her friends, envision for this woman.

'What makes you think you deserve to go to Paris? You think you're special just because you wrote some poetry?' Joel asks.

'I'm a citizen, and I have an annual travel quota. I was invited to a conference, which I'm sure you know is a rare occasion these days, and I didn't want to decline. That has nothing to do with your personal opinion of me.'

'Oh, is that so?' Malcolm says.

A shadow of uncertainty flashes over Marta's face, but she remains perfectly still. 'What are you planning to do?'

'To begin with, we would just like to talk to you,' Joel says. 'Maybe you do deserve to go on a trip. Is there anything you might want to share with us?'

'I told you I'm not involved with any of them anymore.'

'Why, did they kick you out for being annoying?' Malcolm says, childish in his taunts even here.

'No, I wanted to protect my daughter.'

'But surely you still keep in touch with some of them? They were your closest friends for a long time.'

Marta bites her lower lip in frustration. 'You keep twisting everything I say until you've come full circle. I mean it when I say that I don't keep in touch with anyone.'

'I suppose there's no use talking to you then,' Malcolm says.

The silence that follows stretches out for two seconds, three, until Marta turns around and sweeps the child into her arms, making a run for what must be another door at the back of the house. Malcolm pushes past Lily through the doorway, his muddy boots slamming against the floor. Marta manages a couple of long strides before he's seizing her by the shoulders, keeping her tightly in place. She's still clutching the girl, who has started to cry, surprised by her sudden capture.

'I'm so sorry,' Marta whispers to her, almost too softly for anyone else to hear, stroking the child's black curls. 'I should've warned you before I did that.'

Joel's breath is tingling Lily's earlobe as he says 'move,' putting his hands down on her shoulders with some pressure and guiding her to step towards the child. 'Ask what her name is,' he instructs, too close to her skin. She complies.

The girl is quiet for a while. 'Arianna,' she says finally, her voice small but steady.

'Lovely to meet you, Arianna,' Lily says, even though the words feel like acid on her tongue. She still isn't sure what the endgame is here, and the situation feels too volatile. She glances towards Joel, who raises his eyebrows as though to say *keep going*. 'How old are you?'

'I'm eight,' Arianna says, and a beat later, 'Why are you scaring my mum?'

'We're sorry, we didn't mean to,' Lily says.

'But why?' the girl asks.

'It's grown-up business,' Malcolm says as he grabs Marta by the upper arm and Joel swoops down to pick up Arianna. Malcolm drags Marta to the kitchen through an open doorway, Joel close behind with Arianna, who kicks and squirms in his grip. In the chaos of the moment Lily notices evening sun filtering into the corridor, exposing a thick layer of dust on the floor. It's a good thing they haven't wasted time cleaning, she thinks before turning the corner to the kitchen. She sees mint green walls spotted with copper hooks holding wooden spoons and spatulas, sage and parsley in bright blue pots by the window – and Joel holding the child's little arms locked tightly behind her back while Malcolm ties her mother to a kitchen chair with rope he must have carried in his pockets.

Arianna is screaming for them to let her mother go, and Marta is trying desperately to shush her, reassuring her it will be okay. 'Shut the fuck up,' Joel says, while Malcolm gags Marta's mouth with a blue kitchen towel. She looks at her daughter with gentle admonishment in her eyes, but it doesn't work. Arianna opens her mouth to scream and scream and scream again, until Joel turns to Lily to shout: 'Take care of this!'

'What do you want me to do?' she asks, as though she didn't already know the answer.

'Shut her up.'

'How?'

'Like this,' Joel says, his left hand leaving its grip on the girl's arms to snake around her neck, fingers closing around it – she is so small – and then he's slamming her head against the kitchen wall with a sickening sound that sends a shudder down Lily's spine. She is not a stranger to violence as a means to an end, but this feels different, making pain unto itself, wounding deeper and deeper until it reaches the heart of the world, more soft tissue to mutilate. Joel stops and looks at her with expectation. The child is not screaming anymore, but there is a strange sound coming from somewhere else. It takes Lily a second to realise it's Marta shouting through the thick wad of fabric in her mouth. Even if Lily strained her ears, she could not make out the words over the rush of blood in her head, nor let them deter her. Second chances are hard to come by, and so she assumes the role of the executioner without trial, placing her hands over Joel's on the girl's neck. He looks at her with a fondness she has barely ever seen before, strangely intimate, before pulling away and standing back. She closes her eyes and repeats the motions, slamming once and twice and thrice. Each time the impact makes a more liquid sound, the barriers of skin and bone breaking down. The body thuds down to the floor, so light it's barely there. She was barely ever there.

Lily lurches out of the house and slumps down on the steps in front of the blue door. She's been running not on anger, the pure fuel that could keep her burning for days, but desperation, and it's all spent now. *I did it, I fucking did it. I proved that I could do it*, she thinks, hugging her knees while pencil drawings of ghosts dance beneath her eyelids. She sees a woman walking on the street ahead, passing the cul-de-sac without looking at her. Lily wonders if the woman could tell she's a child-killer now, if only she turned to look. Maybe she doesn't turn because she already knows, can't bear to look at her. The blood on her hands is drying quickly, making the skin chafe. The sun is finally starting to set.

The door opens behind her. Joel and Malcolm are dragging Marta by the arms, or the body that used to be her, deep red slashes criss-crossing the linen of her dress. Lily wonders whether they even tried to get any information from her before killing her. It would make little sense to dangle a second chance in front of someone who has just watched her child die. The more she thinks about it, the clearer it is that this is the outcome Joel and Malcolm wanted from the start. She can't think too much.

'Move,' Joel hisses, and she jumps to her feet, surprised her numb legs will still hold her upright. She runs down the rest of the steps to stand on the street. Joel and Malcolm place Marta's body on the lowest step, leaving her in a sitting position. Lily stares at her face while the men retrieve the child's corpse, putting her down on her mother's lap. Joel spills fuel over the bodies and looks at Lily. 'Do you want to light the bonfire?' She shakes her head. 'That's okay,' he says, gently, as though talking down to a child.

Lily has never considered just how much energy is required to turn a human body into ashes. The flames lick at skin and clothes without transforming the shape of them like she was imagining they would. Surely the men know that this is no way to make a funeral pyre. Lily thinks this must be simply another twist of the knife, a way to tarnish what they have already ruined. Save for the sigh and crackle of the fire, the cul-de-sac is oppressively silent. She wonders if the people in the neighbouring house are home, if they have heard and seen their deeds. Nobody will gather to mourn as long as they are there. Even if someone called the police, they wouldn't show: Malcom has given them a heads-up. Lily wants to go home, but cannot speak without revealing her treacherous cowardice, or move without betraying her exhaustion. When the fire finally goes cold, it is already dark. Joel presses his fingers into the soot scattered around the corpses and draws a long jagged line on the blue door, a reversed wave. 'A reminder of what we are here for,' he says. Quelling the tide of parasites. Lily struggles to connect the gesture with the half-burnt corpses at his feet.

When they finally get home, Lily fights the urge to destroy everything she has been wearing, from her blouse to her panties. The acrid smell has seeped into it all, into her core, and she wants to light it up and watch it turn into a small pile of ash in the sink. This impulse is overridden by her reluctance to waste perfectly good textiles. She thinks she should probably take a shower, but pours a glass of gin instead and stands by the window for a long time. The night sky is pitch black, just as it should be. There are still some things that remain unchanged.

'I'm proud of you,' Joel says, calling out to her from a distance. He walks up to her and circles her waist with his hands, rests his head against the back of her neck. Unlike in the darkness of that morning, she cannot feel his arousal now; he seems calm, sated by the successful hit. Being embraced so calmly only makes her feel worse. She breathes in and out, feeling his weight like a tumour on her side.

In the morning, everything is muted. There is no storm outside, and the lights come on as she flicks the switch. Lily gets dressed and takes a detour through side streets already heated up by the mid-July sunshine. Most of the faces passing by look so tired, regardless of whether they are young and smooth or distorted by gravity. She walks past a young man sleeping on the stairs of a shop with shuttered windows, a bundle of plastic bags under his head. 'The police couldn't care less if we take these wasters off the streets now. In fact, they might send us a letter of gratitude,' Malcolm had exclaimed the other day, as though briefing the office of an exciting new policy change. Lily stops and watches the man's sleeping face. She wonders if he is just pretending to sleep, if it is really possible to ever let go when exposed to the whims of others. His face is gentle, sun rays bouncing off a high cheekbone. She looks away and keeps walking, dazed, past tall buildings casting their gentle shadows, past private gardens with their tightly padlocked gates.

There is a small circular garden whose gates have been left open, so generous, what a kindness, and she strides in. The smell of flowers is heady. Most of the blooms have been smashed to the ground by storms, their pink petals scattered like blown-out brains on the grass. Lily thinks she saw a piece of the girl's brain peeking out. Through the blood and the bone, her skull all opened up, with synapses screaming inside.

Lily walks across the lawn and kneels down by a cluster of hydrangeas. The soil beneath them is wet and acidic, rendering their petals an uneven colour of bruises, veiny little galaxies. She feels the dampness of the grass seep through her work clothes, creating wet patches at the knees. She should be getting up and walking the rest of the way to work, but it feels impossibly far away.

Pattern

IN THE ATTIC of an old house on Milkwood Road the makeshift power generator kicks into action, making a loud grinding sound. Mia wakes up with a jolt. For a second her mind is full of white noise alarm, then her body floods with warm relief. *Thank god it's working.* That means they'll be able to use the electric hot plate. Fuel for the gas burner is running low, and they wouldn't have enough bread and biscuits to feed everyone without heat, especially now that the head count has been on the increase.

Jamie and Kadeja are both still sleeping, blissfully ignorant of the metallic whirring in the background. Their bodies radiate gentle warmth, and Mia feels thankful that they occupy the damp cool attic space instead of the living room, where the guests are crammed even more closely together. Come winter, they will all be thankful to have each other at holding distance, although the thought of winter makes a blizzard of fear flash through Mia – who knows where they will all be by then, whether this house will be burnt to ashes, washed away or emptied into prison cells. She stops herself from going any further. Right now, she is present in this house that is slowly, irresistibly waking into a calm summer morning. There are whispers rising from the sleeping room downstairs, the bell-like laughter of children. The only people who wake up as early as

Mia tend to be much younger than her. It's a consistent rhythm of life that got beaten into her at Buckley Street, and she has always been a creature of habit. She stretches her arms in a U-lock shape behind her back before getting up and tiptoeing down the ladder into the hall downstairs. Through the slits in the shuttered windows, sunlight carves beautiful criss-cross patterns into the floor. Someone is snoring very loudly. The worst of the summer storms seem to finally be over.

Alice is already in the kitchen, humming to herself while carefully arranging mismatched mugs in neat rows on the dining table and measuring out leaves into a giant vat of a kettle.

'Good morning,' Mia says.

'Good morning,' Alice says and beams a smile at Mia, making something inside her ache softly. Some people just scatter their heart around like that, their affection so strong it breaks through their contours, colouring in the world around them. It is an exchange of emotion Mia simply cannot partake in. Now that she has entered a space where people are constantly talking about the utmost importance of solidarity and mutual aid and kindness, trying to join these conversations makes her feel like a wretched hypocrite when she's still guarding her own outlines so rigidly. Surely it would be more natural, *better*, to allow one's boundaries to be more porous, to let the light seep in and out and the world wash over oneself.

'The back-up generator woke me up,' she says, as though there is a need to excuse her presence in this kitchen.

'I'm so glad we have it running. We can use the hot plate for breakfast,' Alice says. 'There have been so many blackouts this summer. Sometimes it's clearly because of storms, but other times I'm not sure what's causing it.'

'It might be a transmission issue, although I am wondering if it's systemic. I don't know when they were planning to start switching off parts of the grid, or how permanent those switch-offs would be.'

'Do you think we are on the list?'

'I have no idea. Who owns this house?'

'I do.'

'I suppose it depends how much they know, and how much they care. All we can do is to try and stay prepared. Can I help you with anything here?'

'There isn't really much to do,' Alice says. 'You can help me at eight?'

Mia nods. 'Do you mind if I just stay here for a bit? Everything is so quiet. I like watching you work.'

'Sure,' Alice says, bemused, so Mia watches her finish arranging the utensils on the table. As soon as she's done, she looks up and says, 'Actually, I think we should get some barley porridge started. Let's get the big pan from the shelf above. Can you reach it?'

'Yes,' Mia says, straining on her tiptoes. They set out to measure the grains and the water. It takes ten litres of water to make enough porridge for everyone staying here this morning. Most of them do not have active chips to access resource quotas with, or the freedom to move outside without fear of getting detained, so the volume of rations they get in falls far short of the number of mouths they have to feed. Alice explains that they have just finished setting up a system for collecting and filtering rain water, and they receive some donations. Regardless, there is never a drop to waste.

They leave the grains soaking and go out to the back garden for a bit. After the storms, the earth is covered in mud, leaves and flowers slain and scattered on the soil.

'After all the work we did here in spring,' Alice sighs. 'I was looking forward to the tomatoes, especially.'

'Maybe next year,' Mia says and winces at how hollow the words sound.

Ex machina

THERE ARE CREEPING speedwells growing in little constellations on the side of the football field. From this close, the veins on their purple petals look like scars, even in the low light of sunset. This is one of those moments where everything freezes and you have an endless amount of time to examine every little detail, and that flimsy veil of trivialities will forever dangle over whatever numbed you in the first place. So spellbound, Mia feels the warm dampness of the soil seeping into her school uniform. She worries about what Ms. Davis will say, if she'll scold Mia and make her scrub her laundry clean by hand again. 'You need to be more careful,' she'll sigh. 'We can't be having your school things in the wash every other day.' Mia worries about this instead of the boys barking with laughter over-head, with their sticks and their stones and their stupid insults.

'Fucking sea slug,' one of them says and pokes the small dip in Mia's lower back with a branch of wood. 'Look at you, all shored up. What are you doing here?'

They're always asking her stupid questions she wouldn't answer even if she knew how to. Her fingers are finding little stones of their own, curling around sharp objects in the soil, catching and releasing. The boys are not expecting her to respond, because she never does, and they get what they came for. Just as Mia wishes she could simply sink into the earth, one of the boys seems inspired to speed her along, leaving a muddy footprint on the back of her shirt. Even though the boys are barely bigger than her, the pressure is enough to make Mia shriek in pain, which sends shockwaves of amusement through her audience. Mia isn't always scared of the boys, but now there is a hard fear like a stone in her stomach, a useless weapon. There are some hands tearing at her dirtied shirt and others pressing against her inner thighs. There is the yellow glare of the streetlight illuminating the speed-wells and bouncing off the chain link fence. The world squeezes into a microcosm of the football field by the school, separated from reality, crashing like a comet untouchable by any other agent of reality – how can they do such a thing *here* – until suddenly the gate is crashed by an intruder.

'What the fuck are you doing?' Lily asks, her voice thrumming low and dangerous. 'Get your hands off her.'

The boys comply with such ease Mia is not surprised to lift her head and see a sizeable knife glinting in Lily's hand.

'Apologise to Mia,' she says, lifting the blade.

'She started it,' one of them cries and runs away, and the rest of them follow, except for the scrawny one Lily has grabbed by the blue lapels of his blazer. Mia always sees him tailing the bigger boys. He must be someone's kid brother.

'I'm sorry,' the boy whispers.

'Sure you are,' Lily says, holding the knife very close to his throat. His head barely reaches Lily's shoulders. The sight makes Mia's heart sink from her own throat to the pit of her stomach.

'Please don't do it,' she pleads, squeezing her eyes shut.

'Would you like to do it, then?' Lily asks, taking a step towards Mia and dangling the boy in front of her like a pallid rag doll. 'I think it'd be good for you. You need to learn to defend yourself.'

The boy stares at Mia, and the sight of his huge, fear-glazed eyes makes a shameful surge of pleasure go up her spine. She looks away and tries to force it down immediately. Lily is always picking games Mia cannot play, fights she simply cannot fight, all the while thinking she's doing her a favour.

'I'm okay,' she says, carefully getting on her feet and making a futile attempt to dust and straighten her uniform. 'I just want to go home now.'

'Are you sure? Is that really the best you can do?'

Lily watches her every gesture with a horrible knife-glint in her eyes, and Mia is half-convinced she would stab the boy in her grip the moment her body betrayed its hurt and exhaustion. She leans against the fence and puts a wry smile on her face.

'I'm starving. Let's not miss our bedtime snack.'

'Don't worry, I've got some stuff stashed away from lunch.'

'Please let him go already.'

Lily looks down at the boy. 'Will you apologise to my friend?'

'Of course, miss. I'll do anything you want. Please just let me go.'

'Kneel down and do it then,' Lily says, shoving the boy onto the ground. He scrambles on his bony knees.

'I'm so sorry,' the boy says.

'It's okay.' Mia really just wants to go home. The anger inside her has gone to embers, and this little boy can't rekindle it.

'What we did to you is wrong. I should've told my brother so. It wasn't my idea, I swear.'

'That's not good enough,' Lily says icily.

'Just leave it, Lily. It's okay –'

'It's not okay,' Lily says and, before Mia can even open her mouth, her blade glides through the black fabric of the boy's trousers, tearing at his calf. Lily straightens her back and walks to Mia, grabbing her by the arm and leading her away from the boy who screams and screams and screams into the stifling summer air.

'Why did you do that?' Mia asks, trying to turn back and check on the boy, but Lily's grip is as severe as her silence. 'Aren't we going to call for help? Is he going to die? Please say something.'

'He'll be fine,' Lily says, finally, once they're out of the school gates and the horrible screams have faded into a hideous echo in Mia's mind. 'It's just a flesh wound. Someone will find him soon enough. He'll probably spend his summer holiday on crutches, which is what he deserves.'

'I don't think he deserved that.'

'That's because you're soft.'

'What if I'm not?' Mia says, louder than she intended, and she freezes in the middle of the road. Her hands won't stop shaking. 'I don't even know his name.'

'What does his name have to do with this? I *saw* it, Mia. Do you even know what they would've done to you if I hadn't interfered? None of those boys is innocent.'

Neither am I, Mia thinks, *and that's not the point*, but it's futile to argue. It makes her so angry. Sometimes it feels like the more Lily wants to protect her, the more problems she causes. Now she's kicking up clouds of dust on the side of the road like a petulant race horse, throwing hooded sideways glances at Mia.

'Look, I *know* you were trying to do a good thing,' Mia starts, 'but I shouldn't need your protection, because I'm not a child. And because I'm not a child, I do understand they might have gone too far. I was scared, that's true. But I don't want you to put yourself in even worse situations just because you feel like you need to defend me. It's not fair on either of us.'

'Life's not fair.'

'Do you think Ms. Davis will take that as an excuse for stabbing a boy? Especially when it's not the first time. What if you have to go to prison?'

'I'm a minor.'

'They might still send you off somewhere.'

'Sure. Whatever.'

'I don't want you to go.'

'It's not good if you need me too much,' Lily says, before embracing Mia tightly enough to nearly knock the wind out of both their lungs. 'I might not be around forever.'

'I'm not a fool,' Mia whispers. It's a conversation she will loop in her head endlessly, feeling very much like a fool in hindsight. When Lily cradles the back of Mia's head and pulls her in deeper, deeper, it doesn't feel like a goodbye kiss.

Echo

SOMETIMES MIA REGRETS not going back to the substation to get her things. Throughout her life, her belongings have fit into three boxes – one for books, one for clothes, one for hairbrushes and seashells and various other trinkets. The organisers have given her enough things to wear, but sometimes she misses her copy of *One HundredYears of Solitude* in a startlingly physical way, not unlike heartbreak, or so she assumes. Mia is not sure if she's ever really had her heart broken or not. She realised this when Kadeja asked her about it, on the way back from fixing a broken generator three days ago.

'I'm too hungry to even think about heartbreak now,' she'd said and switched the subject to dinner instead. She keeps dodging Kadeja's questions because every time she tries to dwell on matters of this nature it feels like falling into a deep wet mouth of longing for past, future and present alike, for things that keep slipping through her fingers even as they happen.

The container scavengers have snared a large batch of mackerel fillets in sunflower oil and baby sardines in tomato sauce. Kadeja's elbow keeps touching hers as they work in the kitchen, sorting tinned vegetables into cardboard boxes to be taken away. She can tell Kadeja wants something more from her again, not only to touch her skin.

'Have you ever been on a date?' Kadeja asks in a soft voice, mercifully anticipating Mia's embarrassment.

'Kind of,' Mia says. 'I got asked out a couple of times, back in university.'

'And?'

'And nothing, really. I only ever went on first dates.'

'What were they like?'

'We just talked. It was awkward.'

'I can imagine.'

The comment stings more than Mia wants to admit. 'I really wanted to try, but it's so hard, letting someone know you. And I felt like they were expecting me to be a certain way.'

'They were all guys, right? You had a full scholarship, and most of them were rich idiots. They must have been intimidated by you. For what it's worth,' and here Kadeja's voice softens, whisper-like, sending a shiver down Mia's spine, 'I would've fallen head over heels for you, and I wouldn't have been too good to show it.'

'Please.' Mia nearly drops the tin of tomatoes in her hand.

'I'm just being honest.' Kadeja smiles playfully enough to assure Mia this is not supposed to be an earnest confession.

'How many girls have you sweet-talked into dates?'

'I don't need to sweet-talk anyone. I used to get asked out quite a lot. Recently, though, I haven't had the time to even think about it. Besides, I was never just chasing skirt. I might not seem like it, but I'm actually very serious about love.'

Kadeja stares past Mia's face, looking slightly dazzled, and Mia gets the feeling that she'd love the opportunity to launch into reminiscing about some girl that got away. Mia doesn't want to indulge her with a follow-up question, especially not when there is a risk Kadeja might turn it on her. She would rather keep the romantic futures she has once dreamed to herself. Looking around for a change of subject, Mia finds only dented metal. 'Can you open one of these sardine tins that expired in 2030?'

'Of course.' Kadeja opens the lid, and the smell of rotten fish fills the room. 'We walked straight into that,' she says and laughs. They run into the garden to open the rest of the expired tins, burying spoiled fish beneath the tomato plants. Two children come out, amused by the malodour, and help them with the unceremonial fish funeral. 'It's such a shame,' Mia says, but she is laughing too.

Hiding in you

LILY WALKS INTO the office late, her clothes still damp with dew. It is immediately clear that something has changed in the aftermath of the killing. Everyone appears to be keenly, painfully aware of what she did last night – Malcolm must have made a point of communicating it to everyone – and she sees the deference in their eyes as they look at her. It is clear that her new status as a murderer commands the respect of others, and it would be stupid not to cherish the social capital that affords her in the Party. They had seen her as a half-reformed juvenile delinquent, someone who wasn't a stranger to holding a knife but had never got her hands sticky with blood. Because she'd been recruited due to her association with Joel, it was natural that some people had merely seen her as the girlfriend. Now that Malcolm has passed around the good word – that their protégée has finally got her hands all dirty, that she's a big girl now – she should soak in this newfound respect and fear with a healthy appetite. Isn't this exactly what she wanted all those years ago, when her fingers clenched around bottles of bleach and stolen kitchen knives?

Sometimes you've got to learn things the hard way. That's what Lily has always been telling herself, whether it's about scraping your knees climbing tall trees, or getting hit back twice as hard by your dad, or being told you're nobody's child anymore;

whether it's looking at your hometown for the last time knowing it will be gone forever, or feeling a child go limp in your hands. This latest lesson has been particularly tough, and that's good. That's necessary. She knows she can take it – every single blow she's been dealt, she's absorbed. Sometimes it takes a while to understand what the lesson to learn is, exactly. It's not the method of child-killing that she needed to practise. There was no art to it, just fingers pressing into soft skin, letting the laws of physics and a hard surface do their job. The act itself was over quickly, but Lily found herself faltering in the aftermath, crying on the doorstep as though she had regressed into a child herself. It had stung like a slap in the face, when she had managed to calm herself down a little, take a step back and consider the situation: a government employee hugging her knees, breathing in a desperate staccato, a slime of tears and snot running down her red face. She knows she needs to do better than that, to accept that violence is a means to the end of survival. If her survival comes into conflict with that of some unfortunate daughter of an entitled poet, well, that's too bad. She doesn't have to justify anything, least of all to herself. She's not going to roll over and wait for death. If she can't handle a little killing, she's in the wrong fucking job.

In moments like this, Lily likes remembering her grandmother – always facing away, tending to the gas burner in her cramped little kitchen with green plastic chairs, listening to the radio while muttering curses under her hoarse smoker's breath. She never had patience for anyone, least of all Lily. 'What the hell are you crying for? There's work to do.' That's all she'd say whenever Lily was upset about something. 'What good is crying going to do to anyone?' When she was small, Lily used to resent what she saw as her grandmother's lack of love. She never once hugged anyone. It was only after her death that Lily realised how well and how deeply she'd been loved. It was a rare kind of love, centred in the belief that Lily was strong enough and good enough to do whatever she needed to do. 'Shut up and get back to work,' she'd mutter to herself whenever there were tears in her eyes to be blinked away.

Of course, she has sometimes found herself wishing, shamefully, that she could respond to the hardness of this world with its polar opposite, by letting herself be sweet and soft and infinitely understanding. But that is only an option for those who have other kinds of protection.

'Good morning,' she says to Amelia, who brings her a cup of dandelion tea.

'Good morning, Lily,' Amelia says, averting her eyes. It is a bit of a shock, as Lily is used to being the only person in the office Amelia *isn't* intimidated by. The late morning hours go by quietly. She goes through stacks of applications, finding herself feeling more than reading her way through them. She's in a fatalistic mood, slamming a finished stack of electricians, school teachers, dancers, accountants, and other poor souls whose happiness rests in her incompetent hands on Malcolm's desk, when he and Joel walk into the office. It's around noon, and they seem quite heavily intoxicated. She doesn't say a word to them, just goes back to her desk.

It only takes a couple of minutes for Malcolm to start barking abuse at Amelia. Strangely, it makes Lily feel like one of those mutts that had holes sawn through their cheeks to measure the volume of saliva they'd spew at the ring of a bell. Her own face remains intact, but every time Malcolm's voice bellows through the office, she's sucker-punched by the auditory ghost of Arianna's head being slammed against a brick wall. At least Malcolm is shouting at Amelia instead of her, his ruddy face pushed so close to her pale cheeks that their noses are almost rubbing together. Inexplicably, the sight makes Lily think of the smell of Joel's mouth, the taste of his strangely muscular tongue, ashy and acidic. The bitterness may be the taste of her own humiliation.

There's no way that's an appropriate distance to be admonishing your subordinate from. If it weren't for the sonic waves of nausea going through her, she'd get up and squeeze herself between them. Amelia is clearly unfit for the job – hasn't got the nerves – and her wealth makes Lily feel distinctly un-protective, but she still can't help feeling fond of her. Lily isn't sure if she believes in good and evil, but it seems like an ugly flaw in the world that people like Malcolm see something squishy and get the urge to immediately crush it under their foot.

'What were you on when you wrote this fucking report? My dog could wipe its arse on a sheet of paper and it'd be more informative than this.'

Inside Lily, a sickening reverberation: a bone-dry crunch followed by more liquid sounds.

'Just tear it up and re-do, or ask your auntie for another job. Useless bitch.'

Lily squeezes her eyes shut, but last night's echoes only grow louder. It had taken several seconds, maybe even a minute or two, to kill her, but in her head that whole process is condensed, everything that had been decoloured by the inevitability of death suddenly rendered visible. Now she's overcome by a vivid explosion of details. The girl's mother crying like a strangled animal and then going eerily silent, as if she'd crossed over long before they stuck the knife in her. How heavily the woman's helplessness had hung in the air. Lily had spent years convinced that she could find delight in violence, yet confronted with that direct, skin-on-soft-child-skin violence, she felt sick to her stomach. She remembers the girl's eyes staring at her, wide open, as the men set her body on fire.

She'd felt the urge to go back into the house and find a book to steal, some kind of a red thread to connect them, but she shoved it down. It would have felt perverse. Besides, she couldn't have imagined Joel responding well if she suddenly expressed a desire to read what he would surely call degenerate literature. He draws hard and fast boundaries about the kind of art he considers worth its name, and Lily can never really keep up with the reasoning. It hasn't really been an issue before; Lily's general disinterest towards the arts allows her to evade his judgement. *One Hundred Years of Solitude* is, if foreign, at least classical enough to warrant mild approval.

After Malcolm is done yelling at Amelia, and Amelia is done crying in the kitchen, she floats to Lily's desk like a little ghost.

'You look a little ashen, Lily,' she says, while herself looking downright green. It's no wonder after being spat at. Amelia is smiling in a slightly loopy, wavering way, displacing her own discomfort into concern for Lily. Lily would find it endearing if she weren't so deep in her own head right now.

'Didn't sleep so well last night,' she manages to say.

'I heard you had your first hit.'

'Sort of. I was mostly observing.' There's a flicker of relief on Amelia's face, or maybe Lily is just imagining it because she wants her to be a coward like herself.

'I heard you killed somebody.'

'I did.'

Amelia sighs. 'I wonder when they'll ask me to come along.'

She's trying so hard to put on a brave face, and maybe that's enough to spare her. The boys can smell her vulnerability like a pack of bloodhounds – if she wasn't on their side and from a prestigious family, they'd take their sweet time tearing her apart, as easy as picking petals off a daisy. But she is, so the most they can do is spit in her face for mistakes. 'Shouting at her makes you hard, doesn't it?' she'd like to ask Malcolm, if only she were in the mood to initiate a conversation of any kind. She still relishes the thought, a harmless little hex echoing in her head.

'There's no point overthinking that. They'll ask you when the time is right,' she says to Amelia, as though she really knows what she's talking about, pink cerebrum petals falling over her eyes.

Informant

IT'S SLIGHTLY TERRIFYING how quickly Mia has grown accustomed to Kadeja's proximity. The shell she has spent years growing around herself is more fragile than she thought. Solitude is safer – of course she knows that Kadeja may disappear, or decide that she's had enough of this gentleness. Still, it is blissful to know that she can melt into another body without being pushed away. It has become a habit for them to hide away in Alice's small study after sundown, lying on the warm floorboards, their bodies in parallel, close enough to almost slot together. At some point, one of them will shift slightly to rest her head on the other's stomach, silently asking for her hair to be stroked. There is no urgency to anything they do in these hours, no attempt to broach the boundaries already drawn. They only speak sometimes. Usually it is Kadeja who directs their conversations, and Mia has noticed she likes to talk about her family more than anything else, even though it seems to make her sad. More than once, Kadeja's voice has started to waver while sharing some minute detail about the clothes her mother liked to wear or the places they travelled together.

Although Mia likes listening, stroking little circles above Kadeja's ears while she talks about whatever is on her mind, she sometimes tries to nudge the conversation towards more light-hearted things, believing that wounds often heal better untouched.

Besides, Kadeja has so many fun stories to tell. The life she had before all this sounds like a wild kaleidoscope, at least compared to Mia's monotonous striving to complete one task after another. 'I wish you could've seen London ten years ago,' Kadeja says. 'I don't think you would've liked it much. It was always a shithole. But there was so much life – there was still a feeling that we might not lose everything.' Kadeja doesn't always sound this melancholy. Sometimes Mia worries that the fire in her is going out, but it always shows itself sooner or later.

'We'll get it back,' she says, although she knows it won't draw Kadeja out of this mood.

'Maybe, maybe,' Kadeja hums. 'One day we'll go dancing.'

'We can have a dance in the back garden.'

That makes Kadeja laugh a little bit. 'If only we had something to celebrate.'

Mia is struggling to come up with something – maybe a guest's birthday, or the christening of their new rainwater catcher – when her thoughts are interrupted by a patterned knock on the front door. Her hand stills in Kadeja's hair.

'It must be Nick,' Kadeja says, jumping to her feet. 'I'll open it.'

Mia trails behind her like a pet, unwilling to let her out of sight. Her hand brushes the fabric on Kadeja's back, feather-light, barely there. Kadeja smiles at Mia over her shoulder before unlocking the door. On the other side of the door stands a middle-aged white man in black clothes, sweaty and pale.

'Good evening,' Alice says, stepping into the hallway. 'Come on in. We were just about to have dinner.' The four of them enter the kitchen, where the table has been set with a variety of tins as the centrepiece.

'I was worried about you,' Alice says after they've all sat down.

'It's not me you should be worried about.'

'What's happened?' Alice asks, quickly glancing around the table. A mother admonishes her toddler for refusing to eat the cold mushy peas on his plate; two little girls are whispering something into each other's ears with a flushed intensity. Nobody wants to touch the canned corned beef. The spell of normality is not yet broken. 'Perhaps it's best to discuss this upstairs after dinner.'

So they eat, trying to ignore the uneasy anticipation permeating the air. After the plates are cleared, the organisers gather around Nick in the attic.

'Is it really necessary to be so secretive?' Kadeja asks when Alice closes the latch on the door.

'It's not that,' Alice says. 'Sensitive is the right word.' She looks towards Nick. 'What's going on?'

'Well, it isn't pretty. In the last twenty-four hours we've got reports of at least three incidents leading to civilian deaths that were linked to Party personnel.'

The horror of this news absorbs all other sounds and movements in the room. The room, already quiet, grows even quieter.

'Shortly before noon yesterday,' Nick continues, 'a homeless person was stabbed on the street in Marylebone. It seems he'd got angry at some low-level party agent for pissing in his donation cup – there were multiple eyewitnesses. Got his eyes gouged out and his lungs punctured. Passers-by called the police, but HQ gave instructions to suppress response and leave the body be. That's a marked difference from the spring, when they were at least being sort of clandestine about it. You remember Lottie's case – they kept it very hush-hush and blatantly tampered with evidence, but at least the paperwork was there. Well, that's not the case anymore. That man's corpse was left on the street for hours. Eventually, it was taken to be cremated by some local residents who were worried it would just rot there. Late last night, a woman was murdered in her bed not far from here. A guy broke into her flat and assaulted her before the killing. He called the police during the assault but, as you might expect, no investigation was opened. She was still alive when the lines were open, but just barely. It might have been written off as nothing out of the ordinary, but I did some background checks, and it turns out that the victim had left the Party just a couple of weeks ago. Apparently there had been some conflict between her and one of the perpetrators. She'd disagreed with the policy proposal to cut the rations of second-generation EU immigrants, and apparently was pretty vocal about it in a meeting. He'd got very agitated and threatened to do exactly what he did last night. Finally, a poet and her daughter were killed last night. The bodies were burned on the street. Again, at least one witness contacted the police department, but no action was taken. I believe she used to work with you.'

'What was the name of the poet?' Alice asks quietly.

'Marta Bird,' Nick says.

'Yes, I knew her well,' Alice admits, staring at the ceiling. Despite the slight strain of emotion in her voice, she keeps her calm. Mia thinks it must not be the first time she's received this type of news.

'I'm so sorry. I wish I didn't always come bringing bad news.'

'Do you think the killing was because of her previous involvement with us?' Alice asks as Kadeja rubs her back soothingly. 'I don't understand why they targeted her now. The last time I talked to her, she said she was withdrawing from activism completely. She wanted to protect her daughter.'

'It seems to me that HQ has been supplied with a blacklist of some sort,' Nick says. 'I don't know if they specifically made plans to kill her. It might be more that she was systematically excluded from any protection.'

'Surely Arianna was not on any list. She wasn't even ten years old.'

'She must have been viewed as tolerable collateral.'

There are tears streaming down Alice's face, and Mia feels out of place, suffocating under the weight of emotions she cannot share. If only she were a more open person, maybe she could take this pain emanating from others and let it course through her own veins, becoming the source of something good, a surge of a pure anger that would push her forward.

After Nick's visit, the whispers on the street grow louder; not everyone can afford to avert their eyes from putrefying bodies and corpse bonfires. They receive yet more arrivals, people desperate to seek shelter and, with nearly all of them already being proscribed from access to the public water sources, the shallow well of the few quotas they do have risks running bone-dry. Through some stroke of luck or genius, Jamie finds a contact on the black market, and they supplement their government-approved canisters with crates of Evian and Aquafina. Loading the van with plastic bottles makes Mia feel nostalgic for an age she never even lived through. While skirting disaster, they can feel the targets on their backs growing larger, their resources and bodies stretching ever thinner. The spill of darkness seems to be fuelling the other organisers with an anxious energy. 'We need to fight fire with fire,' Kadeja keeps saying. 'We can't give in to fear.' The same arguments recur every day, about whether it is better to tread carefully in the face of a powerful enemy, whether passivity is the worst kind of violence. Mia catches the tail ends of important conversations. 'We have to increase our horizontal integration with the other groups,' Alice concedes, and everyone agrees, including Mia, although she doesn't quite understand what that entails. Their evenings are filled with hushed phone calls and complicated charts.

In the eye of the storm, Kadeja keeps trying to pull Mia closer and closer. She wants to return the affection, but the gestures feel empty when she mirrors them. There is no urgency to them. She might just as well not kiss her. Mia admires Kadeja's passion. There are pure emotions buried deep within her too – she has felt flashes of them before, fury and lust and maybe even love. Uglier things too, jealousy and greed and uncertainty so bad it makes everything shake. These things are part of her, but they are almost always out of reach, muted.

'Mia, she's a bit shy,' Jamie says sometimes, by way of explaining away her subdued presence whenever there is some sort of conflict or debate at hand. *It's not true*, she always thinks, with something that might be called anger if it were just a bit stronger, strong enough to make her speak up. Instead she bites her lip until it fizzles out. It seems impossible to continue living this quietly for much longer, thinking about torn flower beds and counting all the different ways there are to serve up cold tinned food.

'You have a very sad look in your eyes,' Alice says one evening in the garden. It seems like a strange thing to say, her own eyes still red from crying. At least she has clearer reasons to cry – the people who die are strangers to Mia.

'Sorry.' She doesn't know what else to say.

'You apologise too much – you wrap yourself up in dejection to feel protected. You'd be stronger if you allowed yourself to be angry. I think you'd be happier too.'

Thinking of anger makes Mia think of Lily, who kept getting driven into desperate corners by her rage only to claw herself deeper into them. Mia remembers her with a slightly sardonic smile tugging at the corners of her lips. Lily was whip-thin as a teenager, all stark angles; even her breasts were on the verge of shrinking back into her ribcage. In Mia's dreams her fingers caress the bruises on Lily's skin, get tangled in her hair and pull and pull, and Lily is breathing so tight against her collarbone, still trying to push too hard. They must have been on a collision course from the moment they laid eyes on each other, on a frozen winter evening almost a decade ago. Lily had walked into the dormitory in a hand-me-down uniform at least two sizes too large, interrupting the chatter of the other girls with her disdainful silence. A current of electricity had run through the room, strong enough that Mia was compelled to close her book and draw open the curtains of her hideout bed. Something changed. Lily always had a sharp eye for frailty, and she could tell Mia was the weakest link in the social hierarchy of the foster home. So she did the best she could, weaving Mia a safety net from barbed wire. Mia wonders if she is still alive now, then puts that thought away. There is so much work to do and, at any moment, a new storm could tear away everything they have managed to build. At least that's how it feels, looking at the blooms strewn about the quiet yard. The foundations of all they do are so fragile. When your heart is closed, giving in to quiet resignation is tempting, and surrendering to anger never feels like an easy way out.

Smoking gun

LILY WALKS INTO the corner shop, and all the colours around her seem amplified: red apples shining bright like boiling lobsters, cartons of milk backlit by an otherworldly light. All is aglow with anticipation, or perhaps just the ketamine in her system. She walks down the short corridor and stops in front of a shelf stacked with notebooks and blue pencils. Now that she has outrun the education system, she goes through bouts of strange nostalgia for school supplies. Lily extends her hand and shoves a yellow highlighter pen in her pocket. She keeps walking, making a full loop around the tiny shop. The shopkeeper, a greying Arab man in a chequered shirt, glares at her from behind the till. She glares back. This is the moment. She is floating further and further away from her body, watching herself being watched by the old man, when the tension in her shoulders dissipates. She puts her hand inside her bag and looks him in the eyes.

'I am holding a bottle of hydrochloric acid,' she hears herself saying. 'I will throw it in your ugly face if you don't give me everything in the register. Fucking splash it all over you.'

The man sighs and pulls out a gun. He points it at Lily. They keep looking at each other for a spell, and Lily thinks she has never seen anyone that dispassionate in her life. His brow is furrowed, just slightly.

'Go home, little girl,' he says, and the disappointment in his voice makes Lily's heart clench strangely, painfully. She turns around and runs out of the shop, turns a few corners until she sees Sal and Sean standing in a doorway.

'I would've done it,' she shouts.

'But you didn't?' Sal looks at her, arching his brow. The subtle smile on his lips says that Lily's failure could not be less surprising to him. A flame of anger flickers in Lily's chest at that, but it goes out as quickly as it was incited, leaving her burnt-out and hollow. There is something soothing in being expected to fail.

'He pulled a gun on me.'

'Probably a fake one,' Sean says.

'Yeah, but you don't want to find out the painful way, do you?' Sal says. 'Better luck next time,' he says and pats her on the shoulder.

Now she stands in the dark corridor of the office, shaking in clothes that still smell slightly of the burnt bodies of small daughters with snapped necks, and she wants nothing more than to burn, burn, burn down into the wick of whatever is keeping her together, to see if there is in fact anything there, or if she would simply melt invertebrate.

The needle
and the thread

IT'S BEEN ONE of those nights where Lily can't be sure if she's actually slept at all, the hours stretching into a murky swamp, her body paralysed with exhaustion but her mind unable to shut down. She refuses to give a second thought to the imagery that has filled her mind in those nocturnal hours, and instead dresses in the pale light, leaving the flat without looking back to see if Joel is still asleep. She just knows she has to get up and walk, to ease her overwhelmed mind through the meditation of movement. Even with the blanket of hot air weighing on her body, walking makes her chest feel lighter.

The streets are quiet. It's not strange that most people are inside their houses at six in the morning on a July Sunday, but the absence of familiar figures curled up on street corners is striking. Crossing the Vauxhall station underpass, Lily looks for the girl who always used to beg with her Staffie curled up on her lap. Both of them are missing. Desperate for a mindless distraction, she walks into a supermarket and circles its mostly empty shelves a few times. She shoves a handful of chocolate bars in her pocket before walking out. It's not like she has no money. She barely has to spend on anything, and her salary is higher than average. Old habits are just hard to kill off.

After the terrible void of Westminster, Lily is relieved to see some people resting on the steps and benches. She has a half-formed theory that they're clearing people by the postcode. She walks past a young man who is leaning against a fence, his backpack propped under his head. Half-accidentally, she locks eyes with him.

'Excuse me,' she calls out to him, before she's had the chance to think it through.

'Yeah?'

'Do you know – the government is apparently taking people off the street. I heard they are being killed.'

'We're all gonna die one day.'

'That's true, but you don't have to die tomorrow. It would be safer for you to hide away somewhere.'

'Like where? You do realise why I'm sitting here? It's because I have nowhere to go, miss.'

'What about leaving the city?'

'Sure, I'll just walk to Epping Forest and eat leaves for the rest of my life, probably end up hanging myself in a tree. What's the point? If I'm gonna die here, I'm gonna die here. The government – what good is it warning me about them now? They've already killed me.'

'I see,' Lily says, weakly, and lays the chocolate bars on the ground beside him. It is an act ridiculously, almost offensively, small; Lily half expects him to laugh at her. He doesn't. She keeps walking. His eyes aren't dead. Someone like him, what's he going to do, punch the fence until his hand gets bloody? Jump off a bridge? Take it out on a passer-by who looks at him for a second too long? The whole world is a cage.

'Why were you so stubborn about coming to London anyway?' Joel had asked her, soon after they had met. 'It's so overcrowded.

In a few months' time we'll have slums for people from Aldeburgh, Skegness, whatever. We're already stretched to the limit with the people we already have, including all the immigrants.' At the time, it had made sense, but now Lily doesn't quite understand. If there is such an excess of population, why does it always feel like a ghost town? Is everyone playing a game of hide-and-seek and she's just been left out of the loop?

On her walk back, Lily is so tired she slumps down by the river, dangling her legs above the water. On a day like this, far enough inland, it appears to be an entirely different substance from the one that suffocated her old life and displaced her. There are little lakes of sun within the canal, light-fields glimmering on the liquid surface. Lily gets up and walks up to street level. There is a fast-moving queue snaking around the corner of a glass cube, an old office space that has been designated as a public water point. It's the largest gathering of people she's seen all morning. Some people are wearing their buckets on their heads to avoid sunburn.

At the front of the queue, a heavily pregnant woman tries to swipe her biometric chip on the reader, but nothing happens. At the same time, a young man finds himself stuck in the cube, as his chip won't open the exit.

'What's going on?' the woman says. 'Is it a blackout?'

'No, the lights are still blinking.'

Lily strains her eyes to see the microchip reader flashing bright blue in the sun, twinkling mockingly. There are more alarmed voices in the queue. The man stuck inside the glass cube is frantically trying to force the exit open, but it remains shut. Lily feels certain that the man is going to die. It hangs so heavily in the air. The police will probably have received a notification of the reader breach.

When Lily's own chip had stopped working a few weeks ago, she'd experienced the kind of terror she'd barely ever felt before. She'd tried to refill her flask at a collection point only to see an error code on the screen, 'biometric chip invalid'. The shock of it had almost made her knees buckle, but she'd tried to keep her fear down and walk to another collection point. It had felt absurd. How could she, a civil servant, a born citizen, be told she had no right of access? She'd kept walking with her heart in her throat, thirsty in the stinging rays of late spring sun but scared to take the bus in case she'd be arrested for attempting fraudulent access. She finally found her way to a hospital, was prodded by nurses and told her blood had rejected the original chip. The doctor had eyed her up and down, his own surface glimmering with the oily sheen of sleepless nights and withdrawals. Lily had known he was looking for signs of *foreignness* in her. She passed the test.

In the end, the doctor had slathered a cold gel on Lily's arm and torn the malfunctioning chip out like a used battery, throwing it in the bin in the corner of the room with a loud metallic clank. Lily had looked at the new chip on the nurse's palm as it was prepared for the insertion. It had been just like the old one, a small, grey, completely unmemorable object. A neutral piece of matter. On the way home, Lily had tugged at the bandages with busy distracted hands, pulling and pulling until they finally came loose. She didn't notice she'd been tearing at the seams of the needle scar until it was already bleeding all over the bus seat. It had been dark out and there had been something desperately unpleasant about that sight, the black street ahead, bright ugly traffic lights above, the primordial ink stains on her lap and the seat and the floor. She'd shuddered the rest of the way home, and a fever had risen later that evening, her blood rushing against the grain of the foreign object.

Since then, there have been no problems. The chip is part of her well-functioning body machine, or vice versa, and nobody doubts her right to drinking water. The doctor had no qualms with the quality of her blood. She doubts this man stuck in the cubicle will be as lucky.

Camouflage

THE PAINTERS OF antiquity would have killed to squeeze the pigment of this afternoon sky onto a palette. That's what Kadeja thinks as she stretches herself out in the grass, watching the impossible swirl of colour hang so heavy over the sweltering island of the city. As a little girl, she travelled with her mother to see all the great art museums of Europe. It's the rooms of statues she remembers most often, icy white and frozen in time. She likes closing her eyes and imagining she's walking down a marble corridor in the Uffizi, hundreds of air conditioners humming silently in the background. There is a perfect blue square of light at the end of the corridor, very far away. Before she can walk very far, the grass crackles underneath her like a warning. Mia doesn't stir from her sleep, but her body does, a slender arm snaking its way around Kadeja's neck.

Mia is a little shell, encrusted in the salt of her sweat. In another world, they might be snow crystals. Kadeja presses her ear to Mia's chest and listens to the rush of blood waves inside her. The song's all off-key. They've spent the whole day running around delivering water to unofficial collection points, getting dehydrated in the process. It's a three-person operation: two people to fill and carry the containers, one to watch their backs in case the authorities show up. Nothing makes Kadeja feel as angry as the thought of being done in for this, not even thinking about her parents, who helped put her in this position. When she closed the door of her parents' house on the frozen morning after the election, she didn't think it would be the last time. The more time passes, the more irreparable the wound seems, festering with every summer storm, every blackout, until the pus is more potent than the blood. She thinks of her small child-hand in her mother's hand as they walk amidst the statues, breathing the cold air, suspended in marble.

'I feel like I'm finally earning my place in this world,' Mia had said as they finished their last assignment, her arms shaking with exertion. Kadeja didn't know what to say, so she just pulled Mia's overheated body close to her chest, placed her chin into her hair. It was obvious that the words were terribly sincere and, however much Kadeja disagreed with the idea that Mia needed to prove her worth, any attempt to convince Mia otherwise would have been insufficient enough to be insulting. The best she could do was to stand so still Mia knew she could rest for as long as she wanted to. They'd climbed up the slope of the hill, high enough to see the malfunctioning skyscrapers, to rest in the shadow of trees until the sky would dim again.

Kadeja has been wishing for dark clouds like pools of oil on blue blotting paper, but the sky remains perfectly clear. It curls around the atmosphere like a veiny autumn leaf, mocking them, and she wants it to crackle and fall. Mia breathes slowly, her skin glowing golden beneath its useless armour. A pale red silence stretches on.

Adventure

AFTER THE KILLING, Lily goes through the motions of being a caring girlfriend with a renewed urgency, pressing kisses on Joel's neck in the early morning, making bedroom eyes at him in the office, resenting it while reaping the benefits. It feels important to assure him that murder doesn't make her less of a woman. She keeps her eyes trained on Amelia and mimics her movements, the daisy chain of interlaced fingers preceding a question, the subtle shuffling of feet to signal deference, the incessant twirling of hair. This simple routine works wonders. Joel stops asking for her opinion, cuts her more slack with the paperwork. It could be easy to live like this forever, if only her real self wasn't threatening to burst out at any moment wielding insults and knives. Occasionally, she will glance at the poster of Prime Minister Saskia Bain plastered on the wall above her desk – cold eyes, thin lips, always accompanied by knife-sharp slogans. Although the Prime Minister's strength is not supposed to be her own, she appears impossibly self-possessed. Sometimes Lily wonders whether that means she is not a woman at all or that she has moved beyond the point of having to prove her womanhood.

She has seen the Prime Minister in person on several occasions, each time startled into remembering that she *is* just a person, and a woman at that. That is what it takes to be great at politics, Lily supposes, the ability to conceal one's own humanity. A neat party trick. Soon after being elected, the Prime Minister purged all politically affiliated civil servants and replaced them with her supporters, personally chosen. She ordered the previous Cabinet to be executed for treason, her voice not wavering once during the lengthy transmission. Her eyes grow warm when she addresses her supporters, and a ghost of a smile appears on her lips at times, never quite crossing the line into maternal but giving a faint suggestion of affection. That withholding attitude has a powerful effect; it is no wonder that Lily's colleagues look towards Bain in exultation.

One long afternoon in the office, Joel walks to Lily, leaning over her desk like a big cat. 'I want to buy you dinner,' he says.

'I'm not really in the mood for anything special,' Lily says. There are times she simply fails to make herself malleable. Fortunately, Joel tends to read her hostility as flirtatious.

'A drink, then. Come on, you deserve it.' Joel stretches his body, inching closer until he's at a whispering distance. 'I'm not asking.'

Lily shoots him a look. 'Are you threatening me?'

'I'm not.'

'Who is, then?'

'Someone who wants to meet you.'

'I don't see why they couldn't just call a meeting.'

'They wanted to be discreet and assumed you'd agree to a drink like a normal person. Me, I'm not surprised. Someone will meet you in the lobby at six sharp. Okay, kitten?'

'Or what? I'll be sacked?'

'Are you really that eager to find out? Just go. It's a great opportunity.'

At six o'clock Lily goes into the lobby and meets the eyes of a woman who gives her a little nod. She is dressed in black, a veil of unremarkability over her. Wordlessly, Lily follows her out of the building and across the street, into the silent bowels of the International Trade Department. They ascend marble stairs to the third floor, where Lily's guardian knocks on the door of a meeting room. There are four people inside: a man in military uniform and three unremarkable civilians. Everyone stares at her.

'Good afternoon,' she says, hesitant. Her guide has already disappeared.

'Take a seat, we are just about to begin,' the uniformed man says. He is standing by a whiteboard at the front of the room. Lily sits by a small desk and looks at the other attendees. There's a ginger girl in green dungarees, a tall young man with a ruthlessly receding hairline and a bespectacled woman in a tight black dress. None of them look familiar to Lily.

'This meeting concerns our renewed crackdown on anti-governmental terrorism,' the man in front of the whiteboard says. 'I know none of you are military, so I'll keep it simple. We have invited Dr. Toibin, an expert on left-wing violence and subversion, to brief you.'

The woman in the black dress gets up and goes to stand in front of the whiteboard. 'Thank you. I want to express my gratitude for the work you do to preserve this country for future generations of Britons.'

Lily isn't sure whether she is expecting applause. The small audience remains quiet. Lily keeps her hands folded in front of her, resenting how school-like this feels.

'The anti-governmental terrorist elements in the UK were greatly weakened after the Ebbtide victory in January. Some have been completely crushed by infighting, but others have kept organising at a local level.' The professor stops and point-edly looks at every face in the room for dramatic effect. 'As has been repeatedly proven by history, resource deprivation is akin to oxygen for terrorists, only making them more vicious. It is likely that the diminished local groups are planning to join forces in a national platform, organised both vertically and horizon-tally. Their goal is to destabilise and delegitimise the government by targeted acts of violence. They will almost certainly try to derail strategic policy plans, such as the deactivation of EU-affiliated rationing chips and the launch of new containment clusters,' she says, talking in a breathy, affected voice, and goes on to a lengthy speech about different subtypes of terrorism. Lily's mind drifts elsewhere, only snapping back to the room when the professor makes her finishing remarks and leaves the room, the click of her small heels against marble floors echoing through the door. It all seems terribly theatrical. Lily smiles and immediately feels it is a mistake to do so.

The uniformed man resumes his place in front of the white-board. His skin has the unhealthy glow of a sweated onion, the liquid of his eyes the colour of an overcooked egg white. He coughs into his palm three times before speaking up. 'I'm sure you understand the situation. We are working to coordinate our responses, and every one of you has a key part to play in this. None of you are security personnel, but there are other reasons we believe you are the right individuals for this task,' he says before drawing a messy chart on the board. 'The key group of interest is Weather Underwater, an umbrella organisation of terrorists. They have been implicated in the murder of two Party members last week, and we expect their violence to esca-late in the coming weeks. You have been assigned to a project which we have set up specifically to deal with this threat. You'll be infiltrating the organisation so we can kill their plans in the cradle.'

Lily's chest thumps with tentative excitement. She has been feeling so unmoored from her true self, performing a character she does not fully understand. Whiling days away reading standard-formatted documents, stamping red and blue and filing them neatly only to have her decisions double-checked and frequently ridiculed by Malcolm, is far from what she thought she'd be doing with her life. This is more the job she envisioned when she was first being recruited, and what Joel was selling her, when he suggested she join him in the civil service.

Lily had thought often about Joel's early promise that she would see action, when she was sitting at her desk as the sun disappeared beneath the horizon, finding her reflection shifting out of focus in the dark dust-speckled windows. Most of the time, all she got out of this job was an aching back, tired eyes and a deep sense of confusion. The months following the election had been long and deadening, spring melting into summer, the days growing stormier but no less predictable. Even ascending into the ranks of murderers was sullied by the fact that her victim was a defenceless child, someone who might just as well have been killed by a stray dog. It had been no adventure, just a grim memento mori. In her nightmares it is Lily's own child-self she bashes against the wall.

That is not the whole truth either – the worst nightmares are those where Arianna's body slumps on the ground and Lily looks down to see a ghost she should've forgotten long ago, the waning crescent of Mia's small face. She is used to dreams where she butchers boys who lay a finger on her friend, hides her in a cave by the raging sea to keep her safe from the anger of the world forever. She knows by now that she has no strength to protect anyone at all, but at least this assignment promises some kind of a thrill.

Lily is sent further down the corridor for individual briefing. The pair of officials in the room stare at her with unreadable faces and ask her probing questions about her childhood. They explain that her cover story has to have some overlap with her real past to minimise the risk of slipping out of character.

As the agents go through their list of questions, Lily thinks, *I am a string of information for them to pick at.* The thought is not as displeasing as it perhaps should be. Thinking of herself as a mere set of attributes, an entity reducible to factors such as age and height and gender – somehow it makes Lily feel better about all the messy chaotic things she can never fully account for or understand, her lusts and her violent impulses. So many of her visible features fit comfortably within the parameters of per-fectly unremarkable normality. When she's walking down the street, or asking someone for change, or walking into public buildings, nobody ever questions her presence in that particular space or in general. She always has a right to be there, outwardly ever-belonging. The things that have, at times, cut her off from the society of normal people are invisible – the pain of spiralling out of control badly enough to break the family she desperately wanted to hold together, the heady adolescent arrogance of believing she could devour the world vampirically, taking and taking until there was nothing left to suck but a dry marrow, the strange need to atone through more pain, how it's never enough and only feeds her hunger.

Being seen as a list of attributes is a way of being invisible, holding the core parts of you deep within – because there are no words for them or because they are constantly changing, never fixed in a dictionary form, Lily does not know. There is comfort in that, paralleled by the dread of being seen wrong. She knows she is rotten, in certain moments has even come to embrace the idea, but not in the way the people in front of her think. They insist on drawing fault lines where none exist; the questions they ask are proof of that, poking at her bad-tempered father and overwhelmed mother, the boy she stabbed that got her sent to the orphanage, and the one she stabbed for Mia. But, as she answers their questions, she sees the agents nodding, like she has passed some test, arranging her past into a dazzling constellation of events and assigning a correct emotional weight to each of them. She realises that, though she has never tried acting, if it simply means giving the audience what they want to hear it might not be that difficult.

Now that she has resigned to playing up a role, the words feel more truthful in her mouth. They are buried somewhere inside her. Each retelling of a memory is an interpretation of a dream.

The agents give her an identity: Katie McLeod, only child of teachers in Portsmouth, evacuated to London as her home was taken by the sea, started dating a man of Indian heritage, scared for him and for the future in general now that Ebbtide is in power. Katie has never made big waves in the world, but she's going to the Weather Underwater meeting because she feels that the country has reached a breaking point.

The agents tell her that her assignment is to stay unremarkable and gather as much information as she can about the terrorists and what they're planning; to keep her basic mannerisms and not worry about answering some questions incorrectly, as people contradict themselves all the time.

Back at her flat, Lily straightens her back and makes eye contact with the person in the mirror, a vessel for a narrative. Trying to possess oneself is a disorienting process. The agents had said she shouldn't overthink it, that there's no need to go too far, but Lily has never excelled at following instructions.

Recently, she has been feeling emptier than usual, and this seems like a possibility to fill the void, if only she can follow the script laid out in the documentation.

Even when she was much younger, there were times when Lily caught a glimpse of herself in the mirror and felt a feeling similar to the electric shock of touching another's skin, only resulting from the very opposite of such a sudden caress. At least now she knows exactly who she is supposed to be.

* * *

Saturday morning comes around in a flash. Lily lies wide awake and stares at the dark shadows the sun casts on her naked body, rendering it even more angular. She hasn't been eating very well, even though the office canteen is always packed with food. Maybe it is a form of self-sabotage, letting a hunger she forgot long ago settle back into her bones. She lets her thumbs find her hip bones and draw little circles around them. Beside her, Joel wakes up and immediately rises on his elbows to write something in a little black notebook.

'How are you feeling?' he asks when Lily shifts against him.

'Good,' she says, enjoying the way sunbeams cling to her skin.

'Are you nervous?'

'Not really. I just hope I don't fuck it up.'

'You won't.' Joel grabs Lily by the waist, surrounding her. They are about the same height, and sometimes Joel seems to go through some extra effort to make himself feel bigger, pushing down on Lily's limbs just so, stretching his legs over her body, suffocating her with his greater weight. It doesn't really work. She doesn't feel small, but she can still sigh just so, as though she really were sinking beneath him.

Ticket

MIA IS LYING in her bed and gripping a train ticket in her hand. The thought of leaving for good feels repulsive. For a long time she hasn't felt anything as strongly as she now feels the urge to stay, but leaving is ultimately easier than staying. Soon this city will be completely emptied, a ghostly silence will descend on the streets left ashore and the electrical grid and the telephone lines will die. Although it has never been particularly beautiful, it remains alive for now, and that is how Mia wants to remember it.

She stands up and walks to the window. The dormitory building is low, and she can't look at the sky above the roofs like she used to in her room at the foster house. There she could moongaze when the cloud was light, but now she has to contend with the grey concrete of the tower block beside the dorm. Mia cannot sleep. She writes a letter and burns it above an old green pedal bin. The flame flickers from blue to forest green to blue again and, by the time the words have reduced to ashes, she can't remember any of them.

Just before dawn break, the telephone rings. 'I knew you wouldn't be asleep either. I should've called you earlier,' Lily says. There is a rush of waves over her voice, as though she were speaking into a seashell. 'I was worried I would wake you up, but I should've just trusted my instincts. I'm rarely wrong about you. And nobody knows me like you do.' She is chattering in a desperately hopeful tone, and Mia finds herself unable to say anything in response. She exhales, and the line turns the sound of her breathing into liquid. Lily hangs up when she realises Mia has lost her words. 'See you soon. Don't forget the letters. I love you. Mia doesn't recall them ever writing letters to each other, but the line cuts off before she can ask Lily about it.

She puts on a coat that's much too hot for September, grabs two neatly packed suitcases and walks down to the street. The air smells of sweat and petrol. These streets will form a small part of the bottom of a vast ocean, a mass of water that hides impossible secrets. Mia walks to the railway station with her eyes closed. The journey seems simultaneously much longer and much shorter than it should be, as though she were teleporting but only a few feet at a time, flickering in and out of the familiar landscape. Perhaps she has already become a half-ghost.

The waiting room is packed to the rafters. Mia sits on a narrow bench next to an old woman who is smoking, and wonders what London will be like. She has never had a fresh start before. Maybe the air here has been poisoning her. Maybe it will be easier to be happy somewhere else.

Lily arrives three minutes before the train is supposed to leave and says 'Isn't it good that we got our tickets well in advance?' Her hair is inexplicably long, and she's wearing a blue dress. 'You look beautiful,' Mia says, and Lily smiles and takes her hand. They get on the train that's waiting on the tracks.

As a child, Mia remembers seeing pictures of Indian trains so packed with people that they would all be crushed against one another's sides, sometimes tragically falling off the carriage. Evacuee train 18C, one of the last ones to leave, is not too far from that claustrophobic reality. Lily is sitting half in Mia's lap and talking very close to her ear.

'I feel so strange.'

Mia thinks about it for a while and nods.

'It's difficult to process, that the city we have always lived in could just be buried by the sea and forgotten.'

'Not forgotten,' Lily says. 'It will live on in us.'

'But it feels wrong. It's people that should be temporary, not cities.'

'In a long enough timeframe, everything is temporary. It's not that sad. It's just the way of the world.'

Lily is always so pragmatic. Mia thinks about all the people who are going to stay despite the evacuation order. People who simply do not want to leave, or are not able to. Lonely people who think it's all a bad dream, with nobody there to wake them up to reality.

The journey takes all day, much longer than it should. It's hot and loud, but Lily falls asleep like a small child. Mia looks at her closed eyes, her open face, the chest that rises and falls so evenly. She brushes away a strand of hair that has fallen over Lily's eyes in a slow gentle movement, making the touch as meaningful as she possibly can. Her fingertips brush over Lily's bones, too prominent through the fabric. Now that death is already close enough to smell in the air, does Lily have to beckon it? She presses down on the thin skin, hard enough to leave light bruises like incantations of admonishment, and Lily's eyes open but she is too drowsy to understand why Mia is upset. Mia says nothing.

'What's the time?' Lily asks in a voice still softened by sleep.

'We're almost there.'

Euston station is like a church, so large and open and still inexplicably grim. Mia and Lily walk through the entry hall hand in hand. There are seventeen steps between the main door and the street level, and every one of them feels like a small rebirth.

The air is still hot, still humid, but it feels brighter than at home. The grid of streets is an unknown chaos.

'What next?' Lily asks.

They should give themselves over to the official machinery that has been constructed by those escaping, but they have decided they'll make it on their own. Their desire for autonomy is stronger than any fear. 'Do you remember how we used to slip away through the window at night and walk to the sea, back at Buckley Street?' Lily asks.

'Of course I do.'

They smile at each other and Mia pets Lily's hair that is long *even though she just cut it in a fit of rage in late July, did she not?* Their futures are intertwined as tightly as their fingers.

Shadow

A DREAM OF a Saturday morning: Jamie is reading a book at the kitchen table, stirring sugar into his tea, while Mia draws up plans to install a vertical-axis wind turbine on the roof; some children are pretend-playing to be a bunch of geese, feeding each other bits of stale bread. Kadeja sits cross-legged on the floor, braiding Alice's hair. It's loud, but in a joyful way. Only occasionally the awareness of the big meeting ahead goes through each of them like a lightning bolt, making them frown or bite their lips or shift around in succession. There are so many ways it could all go wrong – if nobody comes, if the cops come, if things descend into infighting – leaving them with nothing but weapons of the weak, fever dreams, self-immolating on the steps of No. 10.

'It's going to be fine,' Alice has been repeating throughout the week, still emanating her usual sense of calm. She has an uncanny ability to make believe that she'll take care of it, whatever it is.

'How many people are we expecting?' Kadeja asks.

'It's hard to say. I think momentum has been building over the last few weeks, but it has been more difficult than before to get the word out and people might think it's too risky to show up.'

'It will be nice to see other organisers, at least. I wonder if Suzanne and Ciaran are still together.'

'Surely not. I bet they hate each other. They always did, really.'

'Let me know if you find out.'

There is a rapid series of knocks on the door. Kadeja jumps up to answer.

'Oh, thank God,' the heavily pregnant woman at the door says as Kadeja opens the door. Her face is bright red and framed by sweaty hair, her eyes glazed over.

'You don't look well,' Kadeja says. 'What's happened?' Others are standing in the corridor behind her, observing in concerned silence.

'My chip stopped working all of a sudden so I couldn't get water, and I can't go to the hospital – I don't know what to do.' The woman is on the verge of hyperventilating, barely able to get each word out in a puff of breath.

'Why do you need to go to the hospital?'

'My water's broke.'

Alice rushes to the woman. 'Let us help you. What's your name, dear?'

'Chandra.'

'Lovely to meet you. Kadeja, let's get her inside. Jamie, can you make sure the bathtub is empty?'

While the two women walk Chandra up the stairs, their arms around her shoulders, Alice turns to look at Mia.

'Could you please go to the meeting instead of me? I'm sure you can do it. It would be good for you.'

It feels like an order, and it's all happening so fast. Mia's body freezes for a split second, but she already knows there is only one direction she can possibly go, so she nods and agrees.

* * *

Lily waits at a bus stop on Mepham Street, absent-mindedly looking at the circular cinema building across the road. It has been turned into a collection point for filtered water, and people stream in and out, holding lidded buckets or carrying canisters strapped to their backs. The monotonous flow of bodies is punctuated by the electric beep of ID chip cards as they slap against the reader. Lily wonders if they will still be here three months, twelve months from now. When things really start changing, they can change so quickly it makes your head spin. *Crush the parasites, sweep out the scum, kill them off before they get the chance to mobilise.* The Prime Minister's speech from last night echoes in her mind. She has heard rumours that they're going to separate the quota levels for ecosystem services even further, introducing a class of subpar citizens above the uncitizens. She wonders if they are raising the quotas for civil servants, military and security personnel as well, to compensate them for the inconveniences of more forceful rule. Lily is unsure what their final victory will look like.

Unable to think very far ahead, she looks back instead, the old cinema building in soft focus. She wants to be kissed in the dark of the cinema, to experience the past as a magnified present, to sit in a room with strangers all absorbed in the same dream. The only films she ever saw were the numbingly boring educational ones presented in civil education class. She knows there was a time when people only went to the cinema to kiss or to escape their life outside, because they all had abundant connectivity to watch films everywhere, even while waiting for the bus. Lily is certain the rich still watch films, the same ones who take their long, steaming hot baths. Their tears must be so pure, so romantic. In a way, Lily is grateful that she will never get to experience so many things – sitting in the darkness of a cinema and hearing lovers pant in the back rows, riding the morning Tube packed with sweaty bodies, feeling the lurch of a plane in take-off. Nostalgia for impersonal memories is a heady drug, and she has no doubt that trying to forge those images into reality would be crushingly underwhelming. There are some things she has already been disappointed by. London, for instance, is not what it seemed to be in her adolescent small-town daydreams: a city of glittering lights and fashionable strangers to meet, an endlessly exciting place of danger and decadence.

'Girls run away to London all the time, bad girls looking for trouble,' her mum had told her when she was six or seven years old. 'They want to have boyfriends, and end up selling their bodies to men that are much too old for them. That happened to a girl in my class.' Lily had mulled those words over in her head for many years. She used to take her mother's warnings at face value, thinking London sounded like a truly awful place – girls selling their arms and legs and perhaps even their earlobes – but the older she got and the more stories she heard from the people around her, the more her curiosity grew. Especially after listening to Sal go on and on about how people in London thought they were so great but couldn't hold a candle to the way they lived, so close to the coast. 'Sure, they have a river bursting at the seams, but that's nothing compared to the ocean staring at you straight in the face every day. They made it all about them for years, but they're never the ones suffering the most.' It had all made Lily desperate to go and see it for herself and, when she did, she was quickly confronted with the fact that the demands of the earth had made their freedom to explore so much smaller, cutting people off from one another via the crude means of geography, and political control had done the rest of the work. Sure, there are more streets to walk down than there were in the neighbourhoods she grew up in, but there is nothing particularly worth seeing. Even though she knows it doesn't make things any easier, sometimes she can't help feeling bitter about having been born into a world so deep in a state of decay that even the parts above water are all contaminated by the stench of the sea, its salty slimy vestibules.

The bus arrives, and Lily climbs onto the top deck, relishing the rare occasion. Buses might be more frequent here than anywhere else in the country, but they're still not a very practical way to move across the city, with its unexpected pools of water and potholed roads. Only walking is. Lily and some colleagues visited the underground tunnels beneath Liverpool Street station earlier in the summer, allowed in by one bureaucrat's engineer brother who was conducting research on the unused network. They were cold and haunted, pitch-black pathways to nowhere.

'Did you know that London has the oldest underground system in the world?' the engineer had said with the cheerful pitch of a tourist guide.

'Was it also the first one to shut?' Joel had asked.

'No, that would be the Shanghai metro. London was the second.'

On a sticky June afternoon, Lily had been grateful for the opportunity to breathe in the cool air, even if it smelled mildewy. She'd imagined it might have been nice to live down here, if not for the fact that one would probably soon go insane from the lack of sunlight and human contact. Access to the network is monitored heavily, with armed police at every entrance. If not for that, these open sections would surely be catnip for refugees and homeless people, with no trains to run them over either. That was something Malcolm and Joel had ruminated about, whether it would be viable to allow lots of 'scum' into the tunnels and then bring in an old six-carriage train to kill them all.

'These used to be the veins surging life through the city,' the engineer had said, betraying his rather poetic nature.

'Is there any way to restore them?' Lily had asked.

'I can't see that happening. Too many sections of the tunnels have been cut off by flooding. The Justice Party invested huge sums to seal those sections in, but the barriers won't last forever, and expanding the network is out of the question when the situation remains so unstable. No politician worth their salt would invest into it.'

'We're in a fucking free fall anyway,' Joel had said. Nobody had the energy to dispute that observation, so they'd stood there in silence, staring at this pitch-black window to the past.

* * *

There are small clusters of people seeking shade under the hot noon sun, faces Lily will most likely never see again, and she watches them sweeping by the dirty windows. It's oppressively hot inside the vehicle, and Lily is starting to wish she had the time to walk instead so she wouldn't show up to the meeting carsick and sweaty. At least there won't be any need to look particularly put-together. She just needs to seem like a regular girl, one who happens to fancy the idea of destroying the democratically elected government of her own country.

Lily has read over the briefing documents many times and cherry-picked the things that suit her. She has stood in front of the window, half a dozen candles lit on the sill, and looked at her own ghost-lit reflection for hours, repeating lines that may come in handy, moulding herself into this person who is – what, exactly? Slightly softer, infinitely more gullible, and definitely easier to get along with than her real self. Joel had been sitting at the small kitchen table, reading some report with his face too close to the candles, and Lily had thought it would be funny if his hair caught fire.

Just before noon, the bus drops Lily off at a side street near an old tube station. Although the clothes she is wearing are light – a loose, blue linen dress with large pockets in the front, perfect to keep her keys and tissues safe, and her usual knife belt underneath – she's dripping sweat down on the pavement as soon as she starts walking. At least the warehouse isn't far from the stop. From her briefing, she recognises the blue panels on the top of one seemingly abandoned large hall structure.

The people trickling in look relatively sane and calm, dressed in ordinary muted colours. No veil of secrecy surrounds the meeting, even though the organisers must be aware that being caught plotting against the government might lead to execution without trial at worst, a very unpleasant detainment at best. For that, Lily does have a sense of admiration for these people. *If you believe in something, you've got to just go for it. You've got to make sense of things in your own way.* As a teenager, she used to say people should make sense of things their own way, just go for whatever it is they believe in, rules and norms be damned. She believed she had unbending principles. Now it seems there is just one overriding principle she's taken to heart, which is not getting beaten in the race towards the bottom. Perhaps that is just an unavoidable consequence of participating in adult society. Even as a teenager, despite all that stuff she thought and said about being free to choose her own way of living and belonging, she was always restricted by her bodily needs, her relations with the members of her group, her need to eat. All that bravado about spinning her own rules was just a sleeping aid. These people gathering to talk about saving the world together, daydreaming while others are being killed left and right, they have principles, and sure enough, there's someone like Lily and her colleagues on standby, ready to drain their lifeblood.

The warehouse space looks like it's being used as a squat. There are mattresses laid in a row against the back wall, dirty plates and bottles of water strewn about the floor. Yellowing plants hang from the high ceiling and the attendees wait underneath, some sitting and some standing, the hum of voices gradually growing louder. There must be about thirty people present, Lily counts, most of them women – young adults like herself, teenagers, even children, as well as a few more elderly people. The men present are mostly older. Lily only sees a couple of people who might reasonably be described as 'boys'. She makes quick eye contact with the other undercover personnel. They all seem to be blending in effortlessly, but Lily wonders if that is because she is not yet used to identifying the subtle differences that set a terrorist apart from a regular person. Before she can follow that train of thought, a short woman with a loud voice starts talking in the centre of the hall, commanding her attention.

'Good day, everyone, and welcome to our first official joint meeting since January. I'm Lydia, an organiser with a Tottenham mutual aid group. Our resistance is needed now more than ever. That is why we have made the decision to merge several existing groups under the revived banner of Weather Underwater.' She looks around the hall. 'How many of you have been involved before now?'

About a third of the hands go up, and Lily makes a mental note of the fact that most of the participants seem to be newcomers. Even in a time of heightened violence, these young women, who she presumes have no blood on their hands, have the courage to attend an open meeting of a terrorist organisation. The lack of security is not surprising, as that's what they were briefed on all along – that it would be incredibly easy to infiltrate a meeting of these bleeding-heart terrorists because they didn't know how to protect themselves in the first place. It's as though they believe that the justness of their cause makes them immune to harm, or perhaps they want to be martyred. It is a painful relief, like the ease with which a child can be crushed to death. Little expenditure of energy is required, but the victory seems unearned.

Lydia keeps talking about a 'campaign of state-sanctioned mass murder', which Lily knows is terrorist propaganda. There is nothing to set her apart from all the other girls in this room, but she feels a strange splitting within herself, recognising the words and not. She glances at the red-haired undercover agent, who returns her gaze with a little nod, an act of grounding.

'We will show this government that you can go so much further with love and solidarity than you ever can with hatred and exclusion. I expect things will only get more difficult from here. Let's look after each other.'

Next, the only male organiser starts speaking, introducing himself as one of the organisers of the Haringey branch and complaining about the recent arrest of some members. As he gestures, Lily's eyes follow his hand and alight on a small, dark-haired woman standing near him, her hands crossed in front of her chest. Lily's mind goes blank. Or, rather, there is a white noise ringing in her head, a surge of cold waves rushing past her knees; layered over this dim hall is the after-image of bruised knees rising up from the water like a pair of bony birches, almost bumping into a softer body so close beside them. A lingering feeling of self-hate from so long ago, a void she has worked so hard to cover up with anger. A soothing voice, a gentle response – 'You can be as ugly as you like, but I hate seeing you all banged up.'

That distant memory of a touch is enough to make her shiver, the way those soft fingers brushed over all the places she was hurting and somehow made the pain feel lesser, even as its intensity increased. Lily had never wanted to stay somewhere as much as she did then, to stop time, but it kept coming in waves, and the walls were closing in on her, leaving her no choice but to run and never look back. And here is Mia, suddenly in the present, strangely an adult. It has been seven years since Lily saw her, but there is no way she would ever mistake that face for anyone else's.

'How many of you have a mobile phone?' the speaker, whose name Lily failed to memorise, asks, just as she is settling back into her present body. A few hands – four, five, seven – snake their way up. Lily doesn't raise her hand, even though her phone is firmly tucked into the front pocket of her dress. There is no point attracting attention to herself or her mobile, which is unreasonably new and expensive for someone like Katie McLeod, recent evacuee and hospitality employee. If she is being honest with herself, she would be physically unable to raise her hand even if that were precisely the thing her mission required her to do. The thought of being seen by Mia right now is debilitating. Of course there is a possibility that she would suddenly glance at her direction and notice her despite the low lights – in fact that is very likely to happen any second now, since the crowd isn't very large – but Lily wants to delay that moment for as long as she possibly can. She supposes the security personnel were unable to access a list of names from a specific foster care institution in another town ten years ago. Still, she feels wronged, remembering what the agents said about the background checks to ensure she would be going into a situation where she didn't know anyone.

The man continues talking about their everyday operations and the help they need, but Lily is unable to switch gear now.

She keeps glancing at Mia's face, then shifting her eyes away the split second the sight becomes overwhelming. It's intolerable, how the mere sight of her affects Lily like a blade to the throat, pushing her heart to her mouth. After doing this three or four times, Lily throws her gaze to the floor instead and strains to keep it directed there. She's terrified of their eyes locking. Now there is a half-formed image that she sees every time she closes her eyes. Mia looks almost exactly the way she did then – same haircut, same absent-minded smile on her lips, same way of shuffling her feet and crossing her arms when she stands, as though she were creating a protective barrier between herself and the world.

Perhaps there is something different about the way she stands, simultaneously more confident and more subdued, and Lily can't help desperately reading into it, trying to find clues about what she might have been doing all these years they existed in complete disconnection from each other. Maybe the posture change signals an important change in her mental state, but then again she must be a little bit taller too, accustomed to her body better than her teenage self. At fifteen, she had been terribly shy, barely speaking to anyone except Lily. Both of them had been better at communicating with touches than words, although that was still not saying much. Lily wonders if she's less fragile now. And then Mia is stepping forward to speak, and she can finally allow herself to look again, as the whole group's focus shifts towards her.

'Good afternoon, everyone,' Mia says. Her voice is still high and thin, ringing clear as a bell with an unchanging tone. Some boys at Buckley Street used to bully Mia for her voice, calling her a drone bird and much worse. Lily has long forgotten most of the things they called Mia, but the ones she does remember still fill her with fresh rage. 'I'm Mia, one of the organisers for

Brixton and surrounding areas. Lydia and Sam have already covered most of the important things. I'm just here to tell you that there is a lot of work to be done on the south side of the river too, and you are warmly invited to join us in whatever capacity you can. If you want to get involved in any of our groups, just come talk to us now.'

How did Mia end up here? It seems absurd – she was always the docile centre of gravity for Lily's violent whirlwind of emotions. Ten years ago, if someone had told Lily that they'd end up being a government employee and an anti-governmental terrorist, she would have expected them to be in the opposite positions. Now, a small group of prospective vigilantes is forming around Mia, and Lily finds her flesh is weaker than the voice in her head screaming she should stay far away. She looks at her undercover colleagues – two of them have joined the northern branch, and the other stops in her tracks and turns towards another organiser as soon as he sees Lily has already joined the Brixton grouping. There are eight of them, gathered in a circle on the dirty floor.

'Could everyone just briefly introduce themselves?' Mia asks with an innocent smile. She glances at the participants one by one, and her gaze gets stuck on Lily for just a split second too long, her eyes widening. She doesn't say a word to indicate that she's made the connection – if anything, it looks like she forces herself to look away and pretends there is nothing to notice. Mia doesn't look at her again. On the contrary, she is pointedly focusing on everyone else in the circle, on whoever's turn it is to speak.

An older woman with feather-light hair is in the middle of an emotional explanation, and Lily realises she has completely missed the beginning of the conversation. She had expected to struggle with playing a character, but this is a problem she had not foreseen, her real self casting such long shadows over the little circle.

'John, my son, he joined the Party during the campaign last winter. To be frank, we haven't been on speaking terms since then. I used to work as an immigration lawyer, and I worry he's encouraging them to target me.'

'Why do you think your son would go that far?' one of the younger women asks.

'Punishing your own family members is exactly the kind of thing that gets you the currency of respect in that environment. He's new and he needs some way to prove himself.'

'Do you live alone?' Mia asks.

'Yes, since my husband died. I got my own power generator installed this summer, so I could sleep with the lights on,' she says with an uneasy laugh.

'If you ever need shelter, please know you're always welcome to stay with us.'

'It's not just shelter I need. I used to be an activist when I was young and I want to get back into it rather than just bouncing off the walls of my house. I grew up accompanying my mother to XR events. Then it all folded, and I thought I'd grown out of it anyway, that it was enough to do my best at my job. Now I don't feel that way anymore.'

The other people in the circle are somewhat younger, all of them women. Lily feels cold sweat drip down her spine as her own turn approaches. She tries her hardest to calm down. People run into their former acquaintances, childhood friends, distant relatives, lovers they never got a proper goodbye with, all the time. That's just life. She never saw her dad again after that one day in April, high blue skies, a figure lying on the sofa in the morning as she was putting on her shiny black shoes and heading to school, then gone in the afternoon, never to return. If she ran into her dad now, she has a laundry list of things she'd like to do, most of them quite violent. She's always liked to think she wouldn't be that sentimental about it. Now, faced with this girl who's not even her family, who she hasn't seen in years, she can't get a grip on herself.

At Buckley Street she used to love sleeping on Mia's belly, feeling the curve of it rising just above her hip bones. She would roll up Mia's shirt and lay her head down just above her navel, listening to the soft thump-thump of her heart. Even that pulse felt so much gentler than her own, as though filtered through a veil of velvet. Lily's heart often slammed into her ribcage so hard it hurt. She grew up hungry, not so much for food but for everything else, perhaps born more hollow than other people. She would bite her nails to the flesh and fight tooth and claw with the world, and that stubbornness is what tore her away from Mia in the first place. She used to dream about finding her again, but now that it is happening it feels like a nightmare, all gentleness extinguished.

When someone asks Mia a question about how she ended up as an organiser, Lily feels an urge to cover her ears and leave the room with her memories intact.

'I studied environmental engineering and worked for the Central Grid for a few months,' Mia says in that voice that strikes deep within Lily despite its thinness. 'It felt like decent work, but the last election made me realise that whatever we do in the so-called environmental sector, it's all in vain if this country insists on cannibalising its own people.' In this smaller group of people, Mia's words flow like water, clear and cohesive. She used to stammer as a girl. Now all that remains of her shyness seems to be the way she holds her body, constantly turned downwards, inwards, behind a shell; but it might not be the bashfulness Lily took it for. Maybe she's just smart enough to not throw herself headfirst into a world full of painful things.

'They asked for my complicity in genocide, and I realised I couldn't take it anymore. Now I just do whatever I can to help, and I ask all of you to do the same, if you can. There are a lot of different things you could do – moving into a branch or helping us on the down low as much as possible, information-gathering, delivering resources, things like that.'

Lily is drifting in and out of the conversation as Mia takes a look at her notebook and starts going over the notes she's scribbled while listening to the introductions. 'Annie, you're a nurse, right?'

'Yes, for three years now,' a young black woman with neatly braided hair says.

'And would you be willing to give up your position to volunteer for us?'

'Yes. My aunt was killed last month. And even if that hadn't happened, it would only have been a question of time until it happens to someone I know, until it happens to me. We're told to turn patients away because they don't look the right way. My job is no longer about helping people.'

Listening to people splash their pain around like water makes Lily feel awkward. They're all covered in it now. Mia goes through her usual courtesies while Lily wonders how many times she has been through this, to arrive at the perfect calibration of compassion and communicative efficiency – writing something in her notebook and moving on to the next person. After going through a few other people's laundry lists of skills and interests, she finally arrives at Lily, staring at her with an intolerable expression on her face. She looks as though she's scared Lily is going to hurt her, as though Lily ever hurt her, intentionally at least. It makes her want to run away again or to do something equally stupid, to crush her mouth with a kiss.

'Could you introduce yourself, please?'

Even if they're staring at each other's faces, they can pretend to be strangers. Lily is willing to play this game – acting a stranger's role is what she came here to do, anyway. But Mia's shoulders are all tensed up and her eyes look too big.

'Yes, of course. My name is Katie, and I'm here because…' she stops and thinks for a bit, bringing her index finger to her lips. 'I grew up thinking none of this stuff concerns me. After evacuating to London and seeing what's going on, this summer especially, I've realised that's not true.'

'What kind of experience do you have?' There is a slight tremble in Mia's voice, or maybe Lily is just imagining it.

'I don't have a lot of experience of anything very useful, to be honest. After leaving school, I worked in my relative's restaurants. That's something I could do, helping in the kitchen.' Lily can barely peel potatoes but, if it comes to that, she's confident enough she can figure it out.

'Absolutely,' Mia says with a smile. 'We're always looking for people who know how to stretch out measly ingredients into a decent meal.'

'I want to do it, but I'm a bit nervous. I've never done anything like this before. Isn't it risky?'

'Everything is risky these days. We are all doing what we do under the threat of death.'

'Surely you are putting yourself in harm's way more than most, though?'

'That's not the way I see it,' Mia says, suddenly impassioned. 'If I was aware of all the problems we have, yet decided not to be an activist, I would be practically suicidal. We are just focusing on the longer term. If this fascist government doesn't kill you, the lack of drinking water will, or the storms and their debris, or the sweltering heat, or something else. Because of my skin, I am already a government target. My existence offends them. None of us are safe – even if you're white, do you really want to drown in the blood of your former friends? What makes you think they'll protect you forever? Any day, they might deem you unworthy. It might seem distant now, but the sword falls fast.'

Lily thinks of Mia's small form curled up on the side of the football pitch, of the way her whole body tensed up when she had to walk past a group of older children. She was always so cautious, and with good reason. Lily had been half-convinced she wouldn't survive in her absence; rarely has she been so relieved to admit her error.

Synapse

'WHAT'S WRONG? YOU look so pale,' Kadeja asks when Mia walks into the living room.

'Nothing is wrong. The meeting went well.' Mia can't bring herself to put it into words. She shuffles her feet silently until Kadeja rushes her: 'Come on, tell me. It's not good to keep secrets.'

'I thought I saw someone I used to know in the meeting,' Mia exhales. 'Someone I used to be very close to, when we were teen-agers. I haven't seen her in years, but I don't think I could ever mistake her face for someone else's.'

'Did you talk to her?'

'I did, but she introduced herself with a completely different name. It was strange.'

'Could it be that she's had to change her name?'

'Maybe. She got into a lot of trouble when she was younger. But I would have thought she could be honest with me, at least.'

'That's tricky. Do you think you'll see her again? Maybe you just need some time to break the ice.'

'She said she wants to come to the meeting next weekend too.'

'That's good news, isn't it?'

'I'm terrified.'

Kadeja smiles. 'Come here. You do look like you've seen a ghost.'

So Mia walks into her arms and lets herself be held tightly, eyes closed, her traitorous mind floating away to places she has visited so many times in her dreams and only once or twice in reality. The sea beach where Mia followed Lily after she'd run away the first time, desperately trying to calm her down. The cleaning cupboard with the chemical smell where the hour of kissing was worth all the headaches that followed. The park filled with white roses where they lay in the grass and let morning dew soak their clothes. All those places she's kept inside her for so long, unable to share them with anyone. What if she dared ask this person – 'Katie', she'd said her name was – if she liked white roses, or if she had ever had a migraine because of spending too long in a cleaning cupboard. Would she pretend not to remember, or could it have meant so little to her that she really forgot?

* * *

'How did the meeting go?' Joel asks Lily as she comes back home that evening, sweaty and tired from the nerves and the long bus ride.

'I think it went well,' Lily says. 'I'll have to gather my thoughts on it for the meeting tomorrow.'

'What were the people like?'

'Surprisingly normal. It was mostly women, mostly younger – around my age, probably. I was a bit surprised there were so few men.'

Joel scoffs. 'Doesn't surprise me in the least. Real men know better than to get involved in these commie terrorist fantasies.'

'I heard some interesting rumours about the Party.'

'I wouldn't put too much faith into anything you hear about the Party in a meeting like that.'

'Well, I'd like to know your thoughts on this propaganda. They said that there are plans to kill people who are detained for having invalid biochips.'

'Is that news to you?'

'Yes.' Lily feels her stomach clench at Joel's casual confirmation.

'I suppose you're not in the policy loop. The details are still being worked out, but it will be something like that. They're planning to detain wasters and stuff them into the empty shipping containers that have been sitting in the Docklands for years.'

'I didn't know that.'

'Is it too much for you?' Joel's tone turns mocking, as though he were ridiculing a child. 'Tough times call for tough decisions. Don't ask if you don't want to hear it.'

'It's not too much.'

'It's true that you shouldn't have heard it first in a terrorist meeting. I wonder who leaked that information.'

Lily shrugs. 'I'm exhausted. I'll just head down for a shower and go straight to bed.'

She lies wide awake all night, thinking about snuffing out all the light that Mia has gathered to herself. She can't expel images of Mia fading away in a container, her bright gaze slowly emptying out. Lily turns over, restless. She knows she needs to steel herself, just like she did before wrapping her long bony fingers around that child's elastic throat. That is her job, to prove her worth in this world.

Genocidal crush

THERE IS NOT a single night that week when Mia doesn't dream of Lily, waking up with after-images of her still burned on her retinas, and they refuse to fade away after she gets up and starts cooking breakfast or tending the garden. Everything she does somehow reminds her of the girl from that weekend, and therefore of Lily, and she falls right back into the rabbit hole of wondering if they will see each other again, if she will solve this riddle that has suddenly taken over her life. It is ridiculous. It's made worse by the fact that Kadeja is somehow hyper-aware of this and keeps pointing it out whenever Mia is zoning out. 'Don't mind her, she's just lovesick,' she'll exclaim to others, and Mia is too embarrassed to protest.

'I never hear stories like this anymore,' Jamie says wistfully.

'But I don't even know what this is. If it really was her, surely she would have told me her real name. What's the danger in it?'

'Don't overthink it,' Kadeja says, gently carding her fingers through Mia's hair as they lie on the floor of Alice's study.

It is pleasant to have lighter conversations after the darkness has stretched out for so long, but Mia can't shake the persistent feeling of dread, balanced on a tightrope between the fear of irreversibly losing something that's become a part of her and the hope of that fragment growing like beams of light in her bloodstream. At least she has plenty of things to keep her occupied. Chandra needs help with her baby, and one new organiser moves in soon after the meeting. It's always unpredictable, reaching out to new people. It's difficult to ask for anything tangible when you can only offer abstract things in return; love and care are not exactly equivalent to milk and honey. Isobel, the hard-luck immigration lawyer, appears at the door on Tuesday morning dragging a leather suitcase full of books behind her. Because of her age, nobody expects her to provide much assistance in the day-to-day labouring with cooking pots and garden shears, nor does she show any interest in such tasks. Instead, she sets out to write a report on the ways in which Ebbtide's policies are violating the Human Rights Act 2040, extant at least in theory. Mia does not quite understand her enthusiasm about the project, even though she enjoys hearing her talk about it at length over dinner, picking up important-sounding terms she has never heard anyone use before. 'We might all lose our heads in the end, but at least we can leave a trace, make it clear some of us were on the right side of history,' Isobel says, and everyone around the table hums and nods politely. In her heart, Mia is convinced that everything will be swallowed by the sea, torn apart by storms, dehumanised. How could it not be? Once the floodgates open, there is no stopping the wave, certainly not with ink on paper. She catches herself using Ebbtide terminology and shudders.

One afternoon, the crackling radio in the kitchen announces that the Prime Minister will be addressing the nation shortly. Mia hurriedly empties packs of shortbread and biscuits onto large plates and places them on the kitchen table to await the crowd of people that inevitably gathers to hear it, as though sugar and butter will suffice to smooth whatever blow they might be dealt this time.

'We have to be realistic,' the Prime Minister begins. 'We have to come together as a nation and build a new, more resilient community. It is with great pride that I inform you I can finally deliver the policy I have been promising throughout my campaign. From this moment onwards, only full citizens will be allowed to enjoy the environmental services of England. Our national ecosystems are rightfully reserved for us, and we can no longer afford to let them be exploited. For those of you who find this hard to swallow, my message is clear: it is time to grow up and understand that our nation is facing extinction. There are no easy solutions. Outsiders will be detained and sent down to the continent, where they will find a more suitable home amongst the other animals.'

'Sent down to the continent?' Jamie repeats.

'A euphemism for the ages,' Kadeja says.

'At least she can't stop them from breathing,' Jamie says.

'I've heard that the plan is to slowly suffocate them in shipping containers,' Kadeja says. 'It's been a rumour around town for a long time. It sounds too crude to be true, which means it probably is.'

Nobody has anything to add to that. They go back inside and make some dandelion tea. Mia feels completely numb. The only thing she can think about without feeling a seawall of despair blocking her mind is Lily's face. It refuses to fade away, but maybe she's not taunting her or haunting her at all – maybe that image is something to cherish with a smile and a secret sigh, something to keep her sane. What does it matter in the end? If there is something to hold on to, it isn't stupid to seek that comfort. It isn't meaningless to feel things just because you might disappear any day now and take them with you.

'I'm sorry for being so distant,' she says to Kadeja in the darkness of the attic that night. They're alone, and the silence seems hard to fill. 'I'm just processing.'

Kadeja is quiet for a while, observing Mia's silhouette shifting against the window.

'Even if it is her, she's not the same person you knew as a teenager,' she says, finally. It sounds like she's given this serious thought. 'She can't be. We all change constantly, chaotically.'

'I'm aware of that.'

'Sometimes it's best to let the past stay dormant,' Kadeja presses on. 'If you never see her again, it might be a blessing in disguise.'

The words twist a knife in an old wound that should be fully healed but, shamefully, is not.

'I know that. I don't need her.'

Starburst

WHILE THE SECURITY personnel claimed that Lily was chosen for the anti-terrorist assignment due to some natural aptitude she appeared to possess in spite of her inexperience, sitting in her first debriefing she can't help feeling they made a terrible misjudgement. Her colleagues have gathered incredibly detailed biographies of the participants in their group, profiling them based on things like their age, gender, place of birth and the shade of their skin. They have memorised the smallest of details mentioned by the attendees, from favourite books to family members. Lily stares at their mouths spouting endless facts with the relentless patter of machine guns, feeling utterly bereft. She barely remembers the names of three participants, including the one who is the root of her problem.

'I got more of a general idea about the people in my group,' Lily says. The debriefing agent scoffs at that.

'We need something we can actually use,' she says.

'I apologise. I got distracted.' Lily knows she should inform them of their serious lapse in background research, but the words refuse to coalesce in her mind, let alone in her mouth. However much she wants to prove herself as a dependable operator, her desire to get closer to Mia overrides all of her more orthodox ambitions. She wonders if Mia feels the same pull; if her wariness overrides her muscle memory.

'We expect you to get as close as you possibly can,' the agent says, as though on cue. 'Join their ranks if you can. Your supervisors have been informed that this assignment takes priority over any other task. Do anything you need to do – within the limits of your power – to gain their trust.'

Of course Lily also knows that the moment she and Mia laid eyes on each other from opposing sides of the dividing line, they were set on a collision course, and every second they spend in each other's company brings them closer to something she'd rather not think about. Despite her best efforts to push the thought away, Lily's mind keeps flashing an endless loop of myriad ways she could see Mia die, or be killed by her own hands. Who is it that shoots Mia in the head in Lily's imagination? Who is it that throws acid on her and sets her on fire? It doesn't matter. All that matters is that she dies, and there will be no point thinking about her any longer. These violent thoughts battle her contradictory urge to caress Mia's face, to press soft kisses on her eyelids.

'There is that strange smile on your face again,' Joel says, as Lily is undressing for bed that night. It makes her jump.

'What do you mean?'

'I don't know, you tell me.'

She has been looking at her reflection in her window, thinking of all the places she used to be bruised that Mia's fingers brushed over so gently, all those years ago. She still remembers exactly where they were on her body – the small of her back, the backs of her thighs, her left forearm. Nothing else has ever made her feel the same kind of electricity.

'I have no idea what you mean. I'm so tired, I must have lost control of my face.'

Joel side-eyes her, but she doesn't care, losing herself in half-real fantasies. She brushes her fingers over that place on the outer edge of her thigh that had been turned into a night-time constellation of bruises by a few boys in the year above. She remembers she had started the fight because she'd been hungry for it, for the marks throbbing on her skin, insisting she feel connected to her body. That self-destructive urge is mostly gone now, but she is feeling indulgent for nostalgia.

'Would you hit me?' she asks suddenly, still facing the window.

Joel's brows furrow in the window's reflection. 'What?' The shock is no surprise, but Lily has little patience for it.

'Could you just –' Lily grabs the hardcover book Joel has been holding, *Can Life Prevail?*, and says, 'Hit me with the edge of this book, just here?' She points to her outer thigh, the site of her daydreams. 'I want to know how it feels.'

'What the fuck? Surely you already know how it feels when someone hits you with a heavy object. It hurts.'

'Yes, of course I know. I want to feel it. Please.'

'Are you trying to frame me for DV? You know nobody would believe you, anyway.'

Lily swallows hard. 'No. That's not what I was trying to do.' She goes to bed and buries herself under the duvet. It must have been years since she last cried herself to sleep. All she sees in front of her now are unexpected, unwanted gateways to the past.

Dawn chorus

THE WINDOW IS small but, luckily enough, so is Lily. She slides it open as quietly as she can, mostly as a formality. Even if someone noticed she's leaving, they couldn't stop her. After the first couple of times Lily picked the lock open, the carers gave up bothering to shut it.

The high night sky is dark blue but, closer to the street level, light pollution pales it into a transparent grey. The air is cool and carries voices of humans and machines, occasionally of screaming sirens. Lily looks passers-by straight in the eye; they react in such peculiar ways. They return her gaze with anger, or fear, or bashfulness, sometimes even with a smile. Most fail to notice her at all. Making contact with others is a brazen act, because most people walking on the street are sealed within themselves. Lily counts two, twenty, two hundred faces, a mass of individuals, all of them trying to avoid being touched by one another in any way. Wouldn't it be great to melt into that mass, possibly even literally, to become part of some great collective consciousness without contradicting motives, without loneliness?

The sounds of the sea and the traffic mix in with bright bird-song, all melding together. The birds are nowhere to be seen.

Lily is standing in water that reaches her waist, wrapped tightly in Mia's arms. Neither of them have said a word for a long time. Here is the connection Lily has always been searching for, the black water rising and falling around them a womb of unpronounceable emotions, transmitting touches that remain at the level of thought.

'Is that how you remember it, too?' Lily wants to ask, but she's too afraid of the answer.

She knows it's foolish to believe there is still some watery bond between them, and yet nobody else can know the long hours they spent by the sea, or frantically cradling each other in the waves, feeling as though their harsh undulation hid them from the rest of the world completely. Other people have their memories of water, but not that, not exactly that. She can still taste the salt, real enough to make her lips split.

* * *

This time, the crowd gathered at the warehouse space is slightly smaller. Lily slips in easily, assuming her role as sweet Katie, the twin she would never be able to get along with. She tries to make herself smile, although it feels unnatural. Lily has always had a face that looks unimpressed, the kind that makes old men go, 'What's your problem, love? You'd look a lot nicer if you smiled,' on the streets, especially when she was still a teenager. She thinks Katie should have the kind of face that makes men just nod and smile in return, thinking everything is in its right place in the world. At the same time, she can't imagine it really works. Surely everyone must see that her softness is a fabrication.

Mia is right there. Lily walks straight towards her, inhaling, still smiling. She's standing next to an older woman with faded blonde hair, listening to her explain something in an agitated way. Lily walks closer to hear what they are saying.

'It was clear from the start that this is what they were going to do,' the older woman is saying. 'It just drives me crazy, that we knew it was going to happen and yet we didn't do anything to stop it.'

'But there wasn't much we could have done,' Mia says in a conciliatory tone.

'That's always the easiest thing to tell yourself. What if it's just not true?'

'Being careful isn't stupid. You've been saying it yourself all year.'

'True, but prolonged inaction is,' the older woman argues.

'We're trying to do something now.'

'But it seems to be too little, too late.' The woman sighs hoarsely. 'Ah, I don't mean to stress you out, Mia, it's not your fault. I'm just so frustrated.' Mia turns around to see Lily standing there, and her face lights up on reflex, but she soon catches herself and defuses her smile. 'I'm glad to see you. Sorry, there were so many people last time and my memory is a sieve – what was your name again?'

Lily isn't entirely sure what the syllables coming out of her mouth will be when she opens her mouth. 'Katie. I'm a woman of my word, you know. I brought my things so I can come with you, if that is still alright,' she says, lifting up a small duffle bag.

'Of course. I'm very glad to hear that,' Mia says and turns away again, whispering something to the older woman, who nods. The organisers from the different branches go through the same spiel as last time, largely unmodified. 'It's been a difficult year,' 'solidarity is more important than ever,' and so on. Mia doesn't speak, but Lily's eyes are on her the whole time. Sometimes she glances back, only to be caught like a rabbit in the headlights, quickly jerking her head back in embarrassment. Lily is not doing a very good job of listening to anything that's being said. After the branch introductions are finished, they follow the familiar pattern of forming little groups. Confirming that the other undercover agents are duly covering the rest of the groups, Lily walks straight up to Mia and Alice. There are five other people standing around them, including one man.

'You haven't changed your mind, then?' Mia says to her.

'Of course not. I'm not afraid of commitment.'

Mia coughs and straightens her back. 'Katie came to the meeting last weekend and said she'd like to join after thinking about it a bit more,' she says by way of explanation. 'I can see everyone else is new. Shall we do a round of introductions?'

'Please.' The older woman, who has introduced herself as Alice, gestures to the person sitting next to her, a young girl with short black hair.

'I'm Maria. I'm twenty, and I had to drop out of uni this summer because my department got defunded. I think everyone's going crazy.'

Mia keeps looking at Lily while others talk. She looks desperate, like there are words weighing too heavily on the tip of her tongue, causing her physical pain.

The only man in the circle, a brown-skinned man with deep frown lines on his face, starts speaking in a carefully considered, clear voice, and Lily wonders if he has practised in front of his reflection too.

'My name is Altaf. I came here with my wife and my eldest daughter fifteen years ago. We had to leave our home in the south of Bangladesh after our house was washed away twice. We could not stand the thought of having to start over a third time. I kept having nightmares where a giant wave suddenly crashed over our house at night and my daughter was swept away from us, into the sea. Some nights, it was my wife. We couldn't stay, and we knew things were so bad in the cities there would be no way to make a living or live at all. People move there already knowing they will be crushed, but nobody can ever be truly prepared for it.'

Lily remembers a sunny afternoon in the music room, Mia's fingers resting on the white keys. They had been given an assignment about their parents' favourite songs. 'I don't even know the name of the place I'm from. The sea just spat me out,' Mia had said, and there was nothing Lily could say to make her feel better. She didn't know a single thing about the music her parents liked either, but it wasn't comparable to the void Mia seemed to carry in her, this small unknown a fragment of a much larger lack. Lily watched her as she sat at the silent instrument, unable to find the melody she was looking for. Everything in Lily's world seems to turn back to Mia now, even others' pain.

'You always think "maybe I will be the exception, maybe God will watch over me, protect me,"' Altaf continues. 'But that is a dangerous lie to tell yourself, and we refused to be tempted. So we sold everything we still had and came here, and at first things were good. I won't bore you with the details, but we really did have a good life here. Some people hated us just for being here, but we did nothing to provoke them and they left us alone. The Justice Party never made us feel very safe, but neither did they threaten our lives. At least they didn't exclude us from housing and drinking water just because we didn't have citizenship. At least they didn't hire gangsters to kill us on the street, in our homes. This year, everything changed. Ever since these fascists came into power we have been living in fear. And this summer, my worst fears came true. My wife was murdered on her way home from work. My elder daughter has disappeared – I haven't been able to reach her for two months, and I fear she is dead too. There is no end to this violence. Where will it lead us?'

'I am so sorry,' Alice says quietly. 'Your burden is too much for one person to bear.'

'But I am bearing it. I am so full of anger – I cannot sit around and do nothing.'

What could be more admirable than bestowing these people with a sense of purpose? Lily thinks, while the city around them keeps gasping for air and only coming up with more filthy water in its lungs. Perhaps she could be sold on it too, were her own position more unshackled. But she knows she can't commit treason, give up her freedom or even her life for these ideas, just as she knows she can't get Mia to denounce them. There is a fire in Mia's eyes whenever she speaks of the wounds carved by this government, and Lily knows she doesn't have the right words to extinguish it. The most she can do is admire her quiet fury, waiting for the moment it burns her too. At least, at last, they can go home together, even if Mia does not know who she is.

'I really thought you were someone I used to know,' Mia says, crammed in the back of a van between Altaf and Alice. Isobel is at the wheel, circling the drowned parts of the city with a steady hand. 'I'm sorry if I behaved in a weird way.'

'Not at all,' Lily says. 'I suppose the way I look is unremarkable. There must be lots of people who resemble me.'

Mia shakes her head and looks as though she's about to say something, but decides against it.

'The last few years have been overwhelming to most of us,' Alice says, ever diplomatic. 'Our memory can play tricks on us. It happens to me all the time. Most often, though, I see something that reminds me of the past, only everything that surrounds it has become completely unmoored. The permanence of certain things only serves as a reminder of transience.' Lily is not used to hearing people speak in such a high-minded way. She finds it quite endearing.

'Does that make you sad?' Mia asks, clearly eager to change the topic.

'Sometimes. But I like thinking of our lives as waves hitting a shore, receding into nothing only to rise again, forever finding and losing ground. Maybe it is just a simplistic coping mechanism, but the idea of time as a circle gives me comfort.'

'I feel like I was born in an era of a dead low tide,' Mia says.

'I agree with Alice. It will pass,' Altaf says, ushering them into an amicable silence. Isobel has turned the radio on, but the signal is bad, and the roar of the engine reduces the classical music to a barely-there wheeze of strings. The sun is still high and the air outside the window sizzles.

Suddenly, two overturned cars come into view to break the monotony of the journey. The brakes screech as Isobel swerves to stop the van from slamming into the wreckage, as the passengers sit in terrified silence.

'Okay,' she says as they come to a standstill on the grassy shoulder. 'It's under control.'

For a brief moment, Lily feels crushingly disappointed that it didn't happen, the easy way out just beyond her reach. After all her catastrophising about meeting Mia, it would've been all too fitting to be killed in a car crash on the way home

'I guess we'll take the A23 instead,' Alice says, and Isobel nods, already manoeuvring the van into a U-turn.

'I never used to be scared of driving,' Isobel mutters under her breath, 'but I swear it gets more lethal every day.'

'Like everything else,' Altaf says, and they laugh. The rest of the drive goes by unremarkably, one parched street following another in a blur.

Mia and Alice give Lily a tour of the terrorists' house, which turns out to be more normal than Lily would have thought. There are no Molotov cocktails being cooked up in the kitchen, no incendiary posters on the walls, no angry young punks posturing militantly. Instead, she is reminded of a more ramshackle version of the foster house: economies of scale in the kitchen, serving up ladles of lentils and gruel; an atmosphere of constant waiting and longing; and, most strikingly, children packed into the living room, whispering to themselves in an attempt to ward off the constant presence of intruding adults. Still, this air is much thicker with despair. Lily can smell the fear of the 'guests' sheltering inside these walls, and she wonders if they can smell her in return. In any case, everyone welcomes her with a smile, except for one of the organisers who eyes her with obvious disdain when she enters the living room.

'Kadeja, this is Katie,' Alice says, and Lily takes a step towards her, extending her hand. Kadeja doesn't take it, instead speaking past her to Alice and Mia: 'Can we please talk in the corridor for a second?' They leave Lily standing in the room, feeling the curious eyes of two children burning holes into her sweat-stained dress. She finds herself tongue-tied, struck with memories of the last time she was in a room with a child.

'Why does Kadeja not like you?' one of them asks, their eyes so big and innocent Lily has to look away.

'I don't know,' she says. 'You have to ask her instead.'

'We have been making enemies too,' the other says.

'With who?' Lily asks.

'The bugs in the cellar.'

Before Lily can get familiarised with the insect life of the house, the organisers return, and she can tell the earlier tension has melted from Kadeja's shoulders. She looks at Mia with a question in her eyes, but Mia refuses to meet her gaze, staring at the floor instead. 'I'm sorry about that,' Kadeja says. 'You are very welcome here.'

Still unsure what *that* is, Lily understands she cannot press it any further. 'It's okay,' she says. 'I'm looking forward to working with you.'

As soon as Lily has set down her duffle bag in a corner of the living room, Kadeja guides her to her new work station, the kitchen. She watches her peel potatoes with a suspiciously shaky hand, but doesn't say anything.

'I promised to do this, but I didn't promise I'd be any good,' Lily says.

'They said you've been working at your aunt's restaurant.'

Lily nods. 'Nepotism, you know. I couldn't peel a potato in less than a minute to save my life.'

'Luckily for you, we aren't going to kill you for that. You'd better have your prayers ready if everyone goes hungry on your shift though.'

Lily laughs. 'Naturally.'

'Let me help you a little.' Kadeja takes another knife and immediately starts tearing potato skins into beautiful ribbons. 'I never worked in a restaurant, but I used to help out in the kitchen all the time when I was a kid.'

'Did you grow up around here?'

'Yeah. Did you?'

'No. I grew up in Portsmouth and evacuated with all the rest of us. I don't really miss it.'

'That is such a funny coincidence. Mia was convinced that you're someone she used to know when she first saw you, and now I find out that you two grew up in the same town too.'

'I'm sure I would remember her. Maybe I have a secret twin.'

Lily is burning with the desire to find out more about Mia. What has she been doing recently? Does she still like to hide under the duvet to read? Is she happy? Who has she become? She keeps her questions unvoiced. There is no justifiable reason for her to be particularly interested in Mia.

'You'd be surprised at the kind of stuff people forget. I haven't seen my mother in so long, I half expect I wouldn't recognise her if she passed me on the street. I wonder how much older she looks now,' Kadeja says.

It might be the company she keeps, but happy families seem rare these days. Most of the people Lily sees holding onto their relatives do so out of desperation, having nothing else left in this world but blood lines in the sand. She thinks she would choose survival over family any day; she likes to think it is a choice she has already made, as though it was hers to make.

'I have nightmares about seeing my mother again,' Lily says, then catches herself. It doesn't seem like something Katie would say. 'Only she has aged into someone completely different, a frail ghost. The thought of her withering away terrifies me.'

'Do you think you'll ever see her again?' Kadeja asks gently.

It is a bold question from someone Lily met barely an hour ago, but she finds it refreshing. For a long time, the mere mention of family used to turn her into a walking wound, stinging with rejection. She felt fortunate to grow up around people who danced around the subject with similar aptitude. By now, her mother is as distant as a ghost from a past life, unable to touch her at all. Of course it helps that the family she is talking about is not hers at all.

'I'm almost certain I won't,' Lily says, trying to put some emotion into her voice. 'They left the coast for somewhere in the Midlands, to live out their lives in as much peace as they possibly can, and I don't know where they ended up or if they're even alive. I tried calling the evacuee registry to locate them once, but I couldn't find them.'

'They're probably fine. We've been trying to locate dozens of people through the registry, and guess how many searches were successful? Three,' Kadeja says with a derisive snort. 'At the same time, we've found some of the unlocatable people right here in London. One of them even turned up at our doorstep after hearing their family was here. The registration system is a shambles.'

'Weirdly, I'm relieved to hear that.'

'Everything is like this nowadays,' Kadeja sighs. 'Just don't assume anything works like it's supposed to.'

'Did it ever?'

'I am sure it can be better than this – people scrambling for the most basic things, being kicked to the curb and left to die on the roadside. You haven't been here for long, in this house, in the capital. When you see how bad it can get, you'll know it's not natural. It never *has* to be like this. If we didn't believe that, we wouldn't be here.'

'How long have you been working here?'

'I've been in the house since we started operating from here. Before that, we ran a co-op in Brixton and I was involved there for a couple of years. It was our base during the election, but after the Ebbtide win we realised it would be safer to get off the registry, become less visible. So Alice let us move into her house back in January. We're in August now, so it's been more than half a year. Time does fly when you're having fun,' she says.

'Things have changed so fast. I never expected my life in London to be like this.'

'They'll keep changing. I don't believe that Ebbtide will be able to hold on to power for very long.'

'What makes you think so?'

'They've been in power for barely half a year, and their violence already reeks of desperation. It's smoke and mirrors for a lack of a real plan,' Kadeja says while peeling the last of the potatoes. 'My parents actually voted for Ebbtide. They thought they'd be protected by the Party, being respectable citizens and all. Well, it turns out that the party doesn't give a fuck about using their core voters as collateral. They'll run out of steam soon and die off like all their predecessors. I don't know what will come next, and I doubt it will be good. At this point, nobody but God has the power to salvage us from this mess,' she continues while working on the turnips and the carrots. Even though Kadeja's words are harsh, the tone of her voice remains light, as though these indictments were just casual small talk to her. 'At least things will be bad in a slightly different way. That's what helps me get up in the morning.'

'They say that variety is the spice of life,' Lily offers, feeling out of her depth. They pile the peeled vegetables on an oven tray, slathering them with a glaze of oil, casually sharing thin slivers of their lives all the while. As Lily settles into her half-truths, ellipses and facts bracketed with falsehoods, she understands why the agents who prepared her for undercover work wanted to ensure the artificial history of her life had sufficient overlap with the real. Even if Katie were to accidentally slip slightly out of the frame, there is a good chance she could remain within her cover with a quick step back. Still, it is surprisingly easy to render her first identity secondary. Filtered through the lens of someone else, the world takes on a new glow.

'Let's welcome our new members, Altaf and Katie,' Alice says over dinner that night, pouring a golden liqueur into the adults' glasses. 'Altaf will be helping us with the new water distribution arrangements, as well as other projects. Katie has promised to take on most of the kitchen duties.'

'Cheers to that,' Jamie says, and someone says something else, but it's drowned out under the sound of two dozen glasses clinking. Having only been to unhappy drink receptions – one funeral and a few stressful government functions – Lily is surprised by how happy she is to hear the sound.

'This is really good,' Mia says about the roasted vegetables. It is the first thing she has said directly to Lily since they got back from the meeting. While she remains preoccupied with her dinner plate, Lily takes the chance to search her face; for what, she doesn't really know. The liquor has given Mia a slight blush, and she looks content, smiling vacantly between bites of food.

'I'm glad you like it.' Lily finds herself reluctant to wade into any deeper conversation with Mia. Even though Mia is the reason she wants to be here, every word they exchange feels dangerous. If only Lily could stay close to her but just out of sight, forever maintaining an equilibrium of short distance. It almost feels possible during the night. Lily sleeps fitfully, both comforted and agitated by the knowledge that Mia is just a few feet above in the attic, hidden in the safety of her dreams. She lies there and listens to the house, and the sound of others breathing around her in the cavernous living room becomes an anchor binding her to the past, time suddenly a whirlwind tearing her into all directions.

In the days that follow, Lily finds a fragile calm in her new way of life. She has to be present, not only to prove that she cares about the work they share, but to perform her real task of excavating information to give to her employers. The challenge is to be silent, but not too silent. So she grounds herself in her new routine, completing each task much more carefully than she usually would, allowing her actions to speak a language of kindness and diligence where words would expose her lack thereof. A small blessing is that the other adults rarely bother her in the kitchen, except to bring boxes of whatever scraps have been delivered by the scavengers or to fetch little cups of hot water for dandelion tea and the like. Instead, there are children constantly crowding at Lily's feet, playing tag or trying to teach her songs, hugging her calves or asking for scraps. She tries to be generous with them, even though she'd rather they stayed away from her. Children make her think of blood and blossoms now, the ugliness of tearing apart flowerlets.

When the children are playing in the garden, or attending the lessons other organisers lead in the dining room, Lily is accompanied only by the radio on the counter. The only channel it can access is One, which broadcasts the hourly news, classical music and educational programming about the state of the world today, except for the one hour each afternoon it plays songs requested by those lucky enough to retain access to phones. She appreciates it as a background hum, but keeps the volume low enough to block most of the words out. For just a little while, it feels good to pretend the faded turquoise tiles and the shuttered windows of this room are the boundary of the world, and there is no need to think about anything or anyone beyond its scope. Perhaps her employers would prefer if she had elected to take on a more prominent role in the group, drawing up plans with lethal stakes like Altaf is doing, but she is happy to blend into the background; besides, politicking would not fit her character. If her bosses wanted her to be more aggressive, they should have given her a different script to memorise. As Lily steals a moment to hide away in the outhouse with her mobile phone, she wonders if the other infiltrators have found a way to be closer to the action, if they are participating in strategic conversations around dinner tables across the city, delegating domestic tasks to the terrorists themselves, picking up Lily's slack.

The phone is the only weapon she has carried into the house. She has been instructed to hide it in her clothes and keep it switched off, save for these brief check-ins. Turning it on already feels like a small ritual. Staring at the cold glow of the screen, Lily grasps for her old self, not far beneath this artificial shell of benevolence. She breathes in and out and reminds herself that there is no time for excuses. For now, all she has to report is the address of the house, the approximate number of people present, and a confirmation that nothing major appears to be planned at present. After sending her quick and likely unsatisfactory message, Lily switches off the device and sits in the darkness for a while, willing her rough edges to recede into a more complacent smoothness again. Walking on the tightrope between her two roles makes her feel restless in a way that is hard to shake off.

When Lily gets back in, Mia is standing at the stove with her back towards the door, making a cup of tea.

'How are you?' Lily says, resisting the impulse to run away and evade conversation. Even if she craves getting closer to Mia, the risk of ruining everything in the process is terrifying. There is so much she cannot say.

'Oh, hi, Katie. I'm good,' Mia responds without looking at her.

'Have you had a busy day?'

'Normal. We're just finalising some plans to install a generator at another shelter nearby,' Mia says, turning around to face Lily. 'I've been getting a lot of practice in remodelling scraps, but it's still a headache. Things always go wrong in ways I can't predict, and I know it's never going to be enough.'

'At least you're doing something.'

'Thanks. You don't have to try and make me feel better, though – I'm okay. I just like complaining.'

Lily wants to ask what else does she like, but she realises the gap between them is impossibly vast now, and the weight of everything she doesn't know about Mia is too much to take on. They stand around for a while, smiling awkwardly and not looking each other in the eye.

'I should get some bread going,' Lily says.

'You've been working hard,' Mia says, suddenly impassioned. 'I've been meaning to tell you. Before you came here, we didn't have anyone willing to take on all the kitchen work, so we rotated shifts with everyone doing the bare minimum. I would usually feed everyone with whatever tinned thing happened to be on hand. You have no idea what a difference it makes to have fresh bread and warm food almost every day.'

'I enjoy it,' Lily says. 'Being here makes me feel calm.'

'It's nice, isn't it? It feels like the hostility of the outside world doesn't reach quite through these walls – although of course that's a paradoxical way to think about it. If the world welcomed us, we wouldn't be scared into hiding, carving out spaces like this just to exist.'

Suddenly Mia's attention is caught by the radio. Standing further away, Lily strains to hear it; when she does, a jolt of panic goes through her, even though she doesn't immediately understand why. It's the time-capsule hour, and they are playing a song that makes her think of black keys dappled with sunlight, Mia's brow furrowing as her fingers map out the sorrowful melody, remembering the taste of stale shortbread Lily used to steal from the cupboards at the orphanage so they could avoid the school canteen and spend lunch breaks in the music room instead. A woman's voice on the radio weaves a velvet blanket over the room, suffocating them with a shapeless sadness that gives Lily goose bumps. Mia never sang the lyrics, but there's no mistaking the melody.

'Do you know this song?' Lily asks, to distract them from the music itself.

'Yes, but I haven't heard it in years,' Mia says. 'I used to be able to play it on the piano. Have you heard it before?'

Lily shakes her head. 'I'm very ignorant when it comes to music.' She can't think of anything else to say; she simply stands there, mortified, wondering if it is only her that is halfway through to a place she's not supposed to remember, until the song fades away. Mia refills her cup with hot water and leaves Lily to sink back into her solitude.

Lily gets her mixing bowl out and beats the dough with more force than necessary, trying to shake the sentimental residue of the awkward interlude. Perhaps it didn't register as such to Mia at all. Perhaps she is simply overthinking. Still, it's hard not to feel there is something like fate at play. Why, of the millions of recorded songs in existence, did they play one of the small handful linking them together? Beneath the fear and the dread of being forced to confront what she is trying so hard to keep at bay, there is a shameful sense of joy, a cosmic vindication – if their bond is too strong to stay dormant forever, so be it! Lily covers the bowl of dough and goes out into the garden while it rises. The clouds are clotting together, threatening them with more destruction. Altaf is standing outside, scowling at them with a cigarette in hand.

'Where'd you get those?' Lily asks.

'Do you want one?'

'Sure.'

They smoke together in silence, cloud-watching. Eventually, Altaf stubs out his cigarette and goes back inside without saying goodbye, leaving Lily to stand there on her own. She relishes the distance. Everyone here has treated her with gentleness, even though she has not worked hard enough to deserve it. Never before in her life has she had to withstand so much careless affection, and it makes Lily feel like she's walking on eggshells, one step away from destroying this strange little nesting-place with bluntly applied force.

Stress
fractures

THE NEXT DAY, while they are all having their lunch of bean soup and bread at the large dining table, the storm hits. Kadeja rushes into the dining room, rain-soaked and wild-eyed. 'Jamie's been detained,' she says and bends over to rest her hands on her thighs, wheezing with exertion. 'We were in the middle of distribution when the cops showed up.'

Alice swears under her breath. 'What about the guests? Did they leave them alone?'

'I think so,' Kadeja says. 'They seemed to just go for Jamie. Maybe I should've stayed to make sure.'

'Absolutely not,' Alice says. 'Do you think it would've made him happier if you got arrested with him?'

'No. But I could've at least tried to make sure they don't do anything to the guests.'

'What would you have done? They are armed and looking for any excuse for trouble.'

'I know. I know. But still. It's so fucked.' She sighs. 'At least the van is okay. We parked in the crescent near the distrib spot, and I left it there for now. I was too spooked to drive back.'

'Good. We'll go back together and switch the plates.'

Lily goes to fetch a towel for Kadeja, who is dripping rain-water over the floor. 'Thanks,' she says, wrapping it around her hair before she sits down at the table. Mia pours her a glass of water, and she takes a long gulp before speaking again.

'Nothing we can do will be enough to prevent this from happening again. I was surprised we got away with it for so long.'

'The Party is not omnipotent,' Alice says.

'But they're not that stupid either. The crowd we draw has been getting bigger every day. They must have taken note of it ages ago, and I'm sure they have a good idea of our rota by now. How can we keep doing it if it's not safe for us or the guests?' Kadeja says.

'What's the alternative? Just sitting it out while people die? You know very well that more and more people are being excluded from the official supply channels.' Lily has never heard Alice raise her voice before, but now she sounds unmistakably angry. 'There is already a shortage of alternative providers like us. If you want to take a break from it, I'll do your shifts. If I get arrested, I can only hope someone returns the favour.'

'Yeah, we could just keep working like this and let them arrest us one by one,' Kadeja argues, her own voice louder than usual. 'If we're lucky, we could maybe stay operational for a few more weeks. Then our guests can find their own money and black market supply, or just roll over and die. Or maybe, just maybe, it's finally time to change our approach.'

'What do you mean?' Alice asks.

'We all know the water scarcity is not as bad as the Party is making it out to be. The situation hasn't deteriorated so quickly because we're actually running out. They're pretending they have to limit access, when really it's just a ploy for controlling the population. You've heard the stories – Party donors have swimming pools in their homes, filled to the brim, and the businesses they favour still have their water mains open. Of course they're trying to keep it behind closed doors, but servants talk even if you threaten them with a slow death.'

'Yes, but we don't have hard evidence of that.'

'Do you actually believe all of this is driven by necessity?' Kadeja scoffs. 'It's insanity, and I think it's time we let them know what we think about it instead of just trying to subvert it. We need to fight fire with fire.'

Lily squirms in her chair, unsure whether she should try to contribute something to the argument or stay silent. Being non-committal feels like some kind of a sin, but she doesn't want to rock the boat now that she's made it her home. The guests look ill at ease about the conflict unfolding around them, pushing the food on their plates around wordlessly. Lily hasn't spoken to them much except for exchanging basic courtesies at mealtimes, but it seems that their status in the group is somewhat muddled. Alice and the others frequently remind them that they have every right to speak up, but they rarely do. Most of them don't participate in the daily work, either because they don't have the capacity or because it wouldn't be safe for them to get involved. Lily imagines the debt of gratitude weighs heavily on them.

'What do you suggest?' Alice asks.

'We should attack a relevant target, say the Ministry of Water,', Kadeja says promptly. 'They're complicit in this, playing with people's lives for political gain. It's already gone too far.'

'But the employees might be like me when I was working for the Central Grid,' Mia speaks up. 'They're just trying to make a living.'

Kadeja shakes her head. 'This is much closer to the government. They've replaced everyone who doesn't support the Party.'

'That doesn't mean they actually endorse the Party,' Mia says. 'Maybe they're just not outspoken either way. Maybe they're just keeping quiet to survive.'

'I think you are being very generous with the benefit of your doubt. You quit your job and they stayed. What does that tell you?'

'I'm not sure.'

'Mia, you know I adore you, but sometimes I think you're very sheltered,' Kadeja says, the frustration evident in her voice. 'Just think about how many people are dying from our lack of action, all while we congratulate ourselves for not using force. Besides, we already have a contact at the Ministry. She is willing to cooperate with us, even at the risk of death. If she's willing to go that far, shouldn't you support her?'

Somewhat reluctantly, Mia nods. 'Maybe there's no better alternative.'

'Whatever else we do, we should still keep up the distribution,' Alice says. 'We'll change the plates, try to minimise the time spent at each location, maybe just turn it into a crate pickup. We can't stop doing it. But I agree that it's a temporary solution, more temporary than I would have liked to think.'

'I think targeting the Ministry is not enough,' Altaf says. 'What about the people who voted for the Party? Do they deserve to live as though there was no blood on their hands?'

'I understand where you're coming from, but we can't kill off every single Ebbtide voter,' Kadeja says. 'And, even if we did, that's not the solution we want. If we must use violent means, they must align with our goals. Poisoning the low-hanging fruit just creates more pointless deaths. Look at what happened to our Haringey branch. Three of their best organisers were executed and the whole thing only seemed to foster more support for the Party.'

'All right,' Alice says, more calmly. 'Shall we do a show of hands?'

Nearly everyone in the room expresses their support for the plan – Lily abstains in silence – and the mood shifts towards the cautiously celebratory. 'Great,' Kadeja says. 'I'll get in touch with Daniella at the ministry and our comrades at the Haringey branch. I know they're out for blood after what happened last week, and they have the materials we need. Now, can I please have a drink?'

'Of course,' Lily says and goes to retrieve a bottle of gin from the kitchen.

'I'm sorry about the interlude,' Kadeja says after having her fill, holding her glass with a white-knuckle grip. 'I didn't mean to raise my voice. What happened this morning really shook me, but I should've handled myself better.' She looks around the table. 'I know I'm the only one drinking, but I'd like to make a toast to Jamie. I hope to God we will see him again someday.'

People raise their mostly empty glasses of water and mumble vague agreements. Lily looks towards Mia and notices she's crying. As if on autopilot, she gets up and goes to place her hand on Mia's shoulder. Mia turns around and grasps Lily's waist, muffling her sobs into Lily's shirt. The lack of reservation takes Lily by surprise, but she understands that people do funny things when they are grieving. None of them are naive enough to think that Jamie will be returned to them.

That evening, Lily is unable to get any work done, lost to a listless despair. She sits on the garden bench, allowing the drizzle of rain to soak her clothes as though it would make her feel cleaner. The fracture between the part of herself which she used to inhabit and the one she is now trying to embody is already festering, filling with a numb necrosis. As long as she can keep it confined to that one part of her, locked away with a secret key, she can still get up and move around, speak as though she is a real person. When she rises and goes into the outhouse, staring at the ghostly blue light once again, she is a fabrication, stepping on a stage slick with blood to perform what she has rehearsed for so long. There is very little to report. As an afterthought, she sends a message to Joel. 'I miss you. Everything is progressing well. I should be back soon.' The thought of seeing him again repulses her. It's not fair on him – she owes him so much – but her heart, ever stubborn, wishes they'd never met.

Lily switches off the phone and returns to the house, but can't quite shake the feeling that she's still in the wrong place. She wanders the rooms in search of a quiet space until she finds a small storage room with no-one inside. She leans against the wall and tries to lose her sense of self in the dust flying in the air, the objects scattered around her, but it is impossible. She should've known that two souls would be too heavy to carry in one body, no matter how strong.

Glancing over the abundance of unremarkable objects held in this room – folders, bundles of fabric, unmarked cardboard boxes – she suddenly focuses on the spine of a sliver-small book balanced atop the mouth of a dusty flower vase. 'STRESS FRACTURES. Marta Bird'. It feels like a fated encounter. The cover is desert-red, with a thick black line of ink dissecting it from corner to corner in an unsubtle echo of the title. The pages are soft and porous, cheap recycled paper, which is still more than most writers can dream of. Lily's heart races as she opens the book, as though it might reveal some great secret that would set her free from her guilt. There is a dedication on the first page: 'For Alice', adorned with a little star inside the soft bend of a crescent moon.

One broken wing is as good as two
My child can't feed the sparrows with her song
In the day I see you in my shadow
Caresses of melting asphalt

Only the night can make us part
Of the same darkness
Held until morning light

Mostly, they are simple elegies like that, half-dirges to a life slipping through one's fingers. Death is a foregone conclusion for anyone, but Lily thinks Marta's poems read as though she had a keener sense of anticipation than most. Not that Lily has much of a reference point. Her knowledge of poetry is limited to a few stanzas she had to read and promptly forgot at school. There are a few notes scribbled into the margins with a blue pen, but Lily can't make sense of the handwriting. If only she could interpret them better, maybe knowing Marta's thoughts would bring some kind of absolution. Instead, every line feels like a new indictment. She shoves the book into her pocket and scrambles out of the storage room, closing the door softly behind her.

Seeking another safe haven, she goes into the kitchen and sees Mia standing there, portioning tinned fish, beans and crackers onto a tray for a makeshift dinner. Lily watches her back from the doorway and retreats into the garden, where the rain continues to beat the remaining flowers into submission. She takes the book out of her pocket and tries to read a few more poems, but the words blur into each other. The rain tangles with the cheap ink, turning the pages into rivers of black sludge. Lily finds a strange, guilt-tingled thrill in destroying the book, like a child sweeping broken glass under a rug. She hears the door open and shoves the wet book back into her pocket.

'Come have some dinner, Katie,' Mia says. 'I hope you're feeling better.'

'Thank you,' Lily says, getting up.

'What are you doing, sitting in the rain like that? You'll catch a cold.'

'Sorry. I was just thinking.'

'It's better not to think too much on days like this,' Mia says.

Everyone else is already eating. It is quiet, except for the baby crying in another room and the arrhythmic clang of metal against ceramic. Someone has lit a candle at the centre of the table, a small prayer.

Ashes to ashes

AT SOME POINT during the night, the rain gives way to a perfect stillness of the air. Mia wakes up in the darkness, suddenly alert, but nothing makes a sound. She concludes it must have been her own dreams that disturbed her rest, then rises to use the out-house regardless. Just before she opens the garden door to go outside, she hears a strange crackling sound, like someone dancing on a dry tree branch, and a flash of fear paralyses her. She has been worrying about their house being found out, struck from the map – surely the target has been on their back for a long time – but she realises the worrying has done very little to prepare her for the real thing. Still, she's had enough of being a coward. She opens the door, thinking she will at least make as much noise as she can if *they* really are waiting on the other side, ready to tear her apart.

There is a lone figure standing in the garden, illuminated by a small bonfire. Mia almost screams, but in the half-light of the flames, she can make out Lily's face, somehow even more unmistakable in the shadows of the night.

When Mia had first brought Lily into the house, Kadeja had voiced her perfectly reasonable concerns – why should they invite this stranger with her ambiguous identity to their table, into the room where their guests sleep at night?

'I know you think it is your old friend, but there is something suspicious about this whole thing. Don't you think we should vet her more carefully? At least ask around a little more, see if anyone knows anything about her?'

'I know who she is. I know her,' Mia had insisted. 'She must have her reasons for hiding her real name. Maybe she killed a cop and had to go into hiding or something – I would not be surprised.'

'Why don't we just ask her?'

'Maybe she's not ready to talk about it. I don't want to hurt her, or scare her. I think she just needs some time, and she will tell me everything.'

'Are you really sure you can trust her?'

'I would trust her with my life – she's already saved it more than once. Please let her stay.'

The words had festered in the air for days, as Mia tried to gauge whether her intuition was true or simply a selfish fantasy gone too far. After endless hours spent poring over that face, wishing she could get her hands on an old Polaroid to continue her investigation without risking exposure, the answer has been handed to her on a silver platter. A couple of days ago, Mia happened to catch the tail-end of a sentence escaping from the kitchen in the wake of loud cutting sounds, 'Katie' forgetting herself while having a conversation with Kadeja – 'I used to live in a foster home for a few years, as a kid. It never felt like home, though. I got kicked out for picking fights with boys.' – incinerating any possibility of doubt about Lily's identity.

That question answered, there are still many others keeping Mia awake at night.

Mia can imagine a whole miserable cavalcade of reasons why she would've shed her old name; slow accumulations of minor transgressions threatening to engulf her whole adulthood, or singular misdeeds so severe she could only run from them by changing tracks entirely. Even if everything else has changed, it is not difficult to see Lily's propensity for getting into trouble as a constant. There are quieter, sadder motivations Mia can imagine. Even if she was secretly jealous of Lily for being a fake orphan, she knew the memories she had of her parents were mostly painful ones. For Lily, having a name chosen by her mother must never have felt like a blessing. The more time Mia has spent imagining such scenarios, the more reluctant she feels to actually broach the topic. Even if the fear that something has gone badly wrong is setting deeper and deeper into her bones, she can't help feeling bittersweet pangs of happiness at the sight of that face so close to her, suddenly present in her waking life again.

In this moment, though, her fondness is overtaken by confusion, the embers on the ground imbuing the night with a glowing dread. 'What are you doing?' she whispers harshly. For a split second, she considers calling Lily's bluff, her tongue pushing against the roof of her mouth in anticipation of the damning consonant. She lets it rest there, for now.

Lily turns to look at her with big, red eyes, and Mia isn't sure if she's been crying or if it's just the bitter ash. Her mouth opens slightly. She looks like a child caught stealing sweets. Mia isn't sure if she's supposed to feel angry or concerned but, in the moment, the former feels right.

'Are you trying to set the house on fire?' she says, walking over to her. To her relief, Mia sees that Lily has planted the fire into a pile of rocks, and the grass is still sopping wet. That doesn't shake her feeling of unease about the whole affair though. She sees blackened strips of paper in the heart of the fire, crumbling into ashes. Lily still hasn't answered any of her questions, but she can't stop herself from pressing: 'What were you burning?'

'A book,' Lily says in a small voice.

'What book?'

'It was my diary. I kept it on me, but it was full of things I want to forget. I couldn't bear to look at it anymore.'

'You could have just thrown it away.' Mia would do anything to read that diary, certain it could have bridged the rift between Lily's past and present self. She realises she has been holding her breath around Lily, waiting for her to reveal whatever dark clouds her old name is cloaked in; sealing it with fire seems like a form of betrayal.

'I'm sorry. I was being stupid.'

Mia sighs. 'Just put it out before anything happens. I'm going back to sleep.'

In the morning, she feels half-convinced it was just an odd dream, but the pile of ashes is still in the garden. Mia stares at it for a long while, as though the secrets bound into the burnt matter could somehow reveal themselves to her, but not a single word remains uncharred. If Lily went to such lengths to erase the words from existence, there is no way she would utter them out loud. And if the flames have purified some dark parts of Lily she refuses to show to anyone else, then Mia wants to be happy for her. Yet the whole episode has left her feeling sullen and scorned. She has never been able to shake the belief that some kind of a special bond exists between her and Lily. She would rather die than admit it to anyone, but for some time after Lily's abrupt departure from the foster home Mia had believed she'd lost her guardian angel. When she saw Lily again in that meeting, she couldn't help interpreting it as something locking back into its rightful place; Lily putting up new walls between them feels more insulting than it has any right to, given that they grew into strangers long ago.

'Katie' is already awake, making breakfast in the kitchen, and Mia wonders if she has slept at all. Her eyes are still red-rimmed, but this time the reason might be sheer exhaustion.

'Good morning, Mia. Would you like some tea?'

'Sure. Thank you.'

'I'm sorry for being so erratic last night.'

'It's okay,' she says. 'Yesterday was a weird day. Everyone was going through some sort of turmoil.'

Lily nods and hands Mia a steaming mug. 'How are you feeling today?'

'I keep thinking about Jamie. But I'm okay.'

'I never really got to know him.' Lily stops, mouth slightly agape. 'Of course I may still get the chance.'

'I don't think anyone is holding out much hope,' Mia says. 'Hoping is painful. I think Kadeja feels the same way. Revenge feels more realistic.'

'Is that why you're going to the ministry?'

'It's not just for revenge. I've come around to thinking that people need us, not just for food and water, but to give them a real alternative.'

'I think that's admirable,' Lily says, her gaze softening with approval. Just like Kadeja's strident words at the dinner table, it reminds Mia of the way Lily used to chastise her for being too weak, too reluctant to take matters into her own hands. She wishes she could ask Lily if she's finally proud of her, and instantly feels ashamed of how much she still craves her approval. In the parts of her mind that aren't dazed by stupid impulses, she can see quite clearly that Lily hasn't exactly made her own life a blueprint to follow, trying to burn her own past like someone else's corpse.

If Lily has really lost herself, Mia does not know how she could possibly guide her back; she's only ever known how to follow.

Like a malicious clockwork, the radio spits out the morning news: 'Nine members of terrorist group arrested in Ealing ... Late last night, the security forces located a cell of the so-called "Weather Underwater", an extreme leftist organisation . . . Based on the evidence already found at the location, the terrorists face charges of treason and attempted murder.'

Although it is all very morbid, Mia can't help but laugh at the timing. 'I guess it'll be our turn next,' she says. 'I hope we get our fifteen seconds of fame.'

'They should at least mention you by name,' Lily says. Mia thinks that is unlikely, since the last thing this government wants is to bestow them with martyr status. They must be portrayed as misguided youths with an appetite for destruction. Still, there is something comforting about the thought of dying in the shadows of infamy. She has never particularly wanted to be seen, or her name to be called. She doesn't think she's suicidal, but self-sacrifice in the name of something much bigger has a different appeal.

'I want to set myself aside,' she says aloud. 'I've never been that important.'

'That's not true.'

You don't really know me at all, Mia wants to say, but the way Lily looks at her makes the words stick in her throat. What does it even mean, to know someone? It could well be that Lily understands her better than she does. It certainly used to feel like that, when they were young. She wonders if Lily would agree with that, and once again the desire to come clean and demand the same from Lily overwhelms her, but the answers to the simplest questions seem the most elusive. Despite lacking a clear point of reference,

Mia suspects she's exceptionally bad at reading people. The actions of others constantly make her feel at a loss. The sight of the burning diary still weighs on her mind, an alien presence. Even if she will never know the truth, knowing that Lily has secrets so heavy they can only be purged through fire is in itself disturbing.

'I'm glad you think so,' is all she manages to say.

Two days before the planned attack on the Ministry of Water, two organisers from the Haringey branch – an angular girl with a closely shaved head and a long-haired boy with a round face – arrive to finalise the plans. If she didn't know that they always dressed in black, Mia would think they were in mourning clothes. She's seen them around a couple of times, but she can't remember if she's ever heard their names, and no introductions are made this time either. The guests want to get straight down to business.

'How many of you still have your biochips connected?' the girl asks as soon as she has sat down at the dining table, and when all of the organisers raise their hands she makes a disgruntled little sound. 'I see. That is a problem. How much of your water do you currently get from governmental sources?'

'More than half,' Alice says. 'But we've been trying to move away from that.'

'You have to. There is no other option,' the boy chimes in. 'We can help you with that, in the longer term. But first, we have to disconnect everyone who is joining this project and scramble their location history. Don't worry, we have the tools to make it almost completely painless.'

'We trust you,' Kadeja says.

'Next, let's talk about the game plan. You don't have to worry about the ammo,' the girl says, spreading out a map on the table. She circles a quiet side road in blue. 'We'll meet here at 10am on the day. You just have to take care of the driving. Kadeja, have you confirmed that your contact will be waiting for us?'

'Yes. We'll give Daniella the bag, and she will take it into the staff canteen. It will be set to detonate at 12.30pm, which is when most of the employees will be taking their lunch.'

'How much do you trust her?'

'Almost completely.'

Nobody mentions the myriad other things that could go wrong; at this point, it's all a Hail Mary.

Lily enters the dining room to bring them some freshly baked bread, and the Haringey organisers proceed to tell woeful stories of surviving on half-rotten food scavenged from bins. Apparently their operation is smaller, more focused on trying to disrupt the workings of the Party; with no guests to take care of, they are neglecting care of themselves.

'You should have dinner with us sometime,' Kadeja says. 'Katie does an excellent job with what she gets from the scavengers.'

'After the assignment,' the boy says, 'we will definitely take you up on that offer.'

They iron out the rest of the important details before departing, one of them carrying a loaf of sourdough underarm.

It is a bright, beautiful day, and the air carries the sweet smell of a fully ripened summer. Mia has always loved this time of year, and dreaded it too; it is perfect, yet will soon cross the tipping point into the rotting season, decay like vomit in the air. With the current state of the sanitation system, the streets have a fragrance of the open sewer more often than not. Mia is convinced that it's yet another disaster waiting to happen, but one that feels barely worth mentioning, what with every other plague blighting them.

'I can sense a growing bloodlust amongst our group,' Isobel

says to her while they're moving the outhouse sludge to the compost pile in the back of the garden. 'I don't like it.'

'What do you mean?'

'All my life, I've heard arguments about violence being a necessary evil, but I'm still not convinced. Are you? I never took you for a violent person.'

Mia sighs. 'Me neither.'

'Will you go with them?'

'Yes. We've got to do something more than we've been doing.'

'But why is this the thing that needs doing? Whatever motions we set forth in this world will continue on their paths long after we are gone. Violence will only breed violence.'

'We're not talking about rabbits. And if you really want to apply this genealogical analysis to history, don't you think peace seems like a recessive gene? You can't breed anything in isolation.' Mia suspects she sounds far more convinced than she really is, but that still feels like a step forward.

'Fine,' Isobel says, putting the empty pail back into the latrine with a clang. 'I don't see how this plan is going to change anything for the better, and I wish you wouldn't go get yourself killed in the process of murder. But we all have to make our own mistakes.'

'Maybe we are like rabid animals, cornered in a cage – but surely it is better to go out with a fight,' Mia says. It is strange how desperation can melt the complicated tensions of life into such simplistic axioms.

* * *

On the morning of the planned attack, Mia and Kadeja wake early and have tea in the garden. Mia's hands are shaking around the handle of her cup, and she hopes Kadeja doesn't notice.

'You seem so nervous,' Kadeja says, dashing her wishes.

'I just feel like I'm teetering on the brink of something, and I'm not sure if it's good or bad.'

'It will be fine. If everything goes to plan, we'll come back home and have dinner. And nothing will change, except for people hopefully seeing that the Party is far from infallible.'

'I really hope so.'

Kadeja takes hold of her hand, and the touch feels grounding. Mia's heart feels full with gratitude for Kadeja, all the protection she has received, but the only way she can express it is by gripping her fingers a little tighter.

'Is that Morse code?' Kadeja jokes gently.

'No, unless you want it to be. What am I saying?'

'I'll keep it to myself.' Kadeja smiles at her without gravity, and it makes Mia laugh with an almost childlike joy. She never knew what it was like to be teased while being in on the joke. She gives Kadeja's hand another pulse and lets it go.

She feels like she could with equal ease say something poignant or simply remain silent. It is impossible to deny that there is a sense of foreboding in every movement, every gaze they exchange, making it all seem more meaningful than it has any right to be. If their mission fails, there will be little time to care about what-ifs; if it succeeds, the urgency of this moment will be lost in hindsight, demoted to mundanity.

While their cups of tea are still half-full, Lily enters the room.

'What's wrong?' Kadeja asks after taking one look at her face.

'The generator — I can hear it all the way from the living room. I think there's something wrong with it.'

'Oh,' Mia says, already jumping out of her chair. 'I'll take a look.'

'Are you sure this can't wait until we're back?' Kadeja asks.

'We might not come back,' Mia says, and although the words sound overly dramatic to her own ears, she knows they are true. 'And it seems like a storm is gathering. If there's a long power cut while the generator isn't working and we are gone – everyone left here will struggle to feed themselves.'

'You're overthinking it,' Kadeja says. 'I'm sure they'll be fine. And so will we.'

'It's my responsibility. Maybe there's a quick fix. I'll go have a look.'

As soon as Mia enters the living room and hears the noise from the attic, she knows there is *something wrong*, that all-too-familiar sinking-stomach feeling. Her brain soon catches up with her gut. Although the generator should not be switched on at all, it is making a wheezing grind on the other side of the wall, a chain smoker's lung about to give out. She curses under her breath and rushes to the flat roof terrace, with Kadeja following closely behind her.

'What is it?'

'I'll have to look at it to know more.'

'We have to go in fifteen minutes. Are you sure you want to do this?'

Lily emerges from the attic, standing over the generator with a mournful air. 'I really don't think any of us knows what to do with this.'

'Is it really that urgent?' Kadeja asks, taking a step towards Lily.

'We have to heat up water to clean Baby's things – and I don't have enough processed foods in the kitchen to feed us for more than a couple of days,' Lily says.

'I get that,' Kadeja says, deflated. 'I get that it's not ideal.' She turns towards Mia, who is kneeling by the generator, staring at its exposed innards after having removed the side panel. 'But I really don't want to go without you.'

'It'll be fine, I swear it'll be fine,' Mia says, mostly to convince herself. It doesn't work.

The minutes Mia spends kneeling by the overheated generator, both Kadeja's and Lily's eyes burning holes into the back of her head, are some of the most agonising of her entire life. After a blink of an eye, or an eternity, Kadeja kneels down beside her. 'I've got to go now,' she says, breaking the tension somewhat. 'Are you sure you don't want to give it a rest?'

'I want to,', Mia says, fighting back tears of frustration. 'But I have to fix this.' She feels like she is making a mistake, but it still feels important. 'We should apply our skills where they are most needed,' she adds, weakly.

'I don't have time to argue with you,', Kadeja says, pulling Mia in for a hug. 'It's enough if me and the Haringey organisers are there. We just have to support Daniella.'

'Yeah,' Mia mutters into Kadeja's shirt.

'I'll see you in a few hours.'

'See you. Good luck.'

Mia watches Kadeja disappear into the attic. Lily watches her also, but doesn't say a thing. Mia sees them looking at each other with something ugly in their eyes, but she is too overwhelmed to give it another thought.

Around noon, the sky goes black, and she's no closer to diagnosing the problem, let alone fixing it. Mia wants to tear her hair out in frustration. Instead, she slides the side panel of the generator shut and slumps onto the concrete floor. She thinks of the bomb the Haringey crew will have brought to the ministry, dormant in a sleek black suitcase, a moment of calm before the artificial storm followed by pieces of shrapnel and plastic flying in all directions. The clouds above her coagulate into an omen, one that will grow talons like a murder of crows raining destruction upon the world beneath. The thunder is going to hit any moment now, and all the electricity crackling in the air is going to go cold and dead, a stone breast. The urge to run away nearly overcomes her, but she lets gravity keep her in its grip, close against the hard surface.

Mia closes her eyes and imagines Kadeja lying down beside her, stroking her palm with steady fingers, pulsating a constant warmth. She drifts deeper into the image, turning onto her side, and suddenly it's Lily's eyes she's staring at, wide and watery.

Thunder.

'What did you say?'

It takes her a moment to realise that Lily is standing above her, asking her a question.

'Nothing,' Mia says, rubbing her eyes. Maybe it's because the foundations she has built her present on will not stop trembling, but a sliver of doubt snakes into her mind like a cruel sunbeam. She's certain Lily's were glacier-blue, impenetrable in their lightness, always reflecting her own insecurities right back at her; the irises she is staring at are a brown-speckled green, absorbing her current confusion in a reassuring way. Her chest tightens, but she can't name the feeling. It is frightening to realise she doesn't know what she wants anymore; whether there is anything left to truly want.

'Sorry' Mia says. 'I was half-asleep.'

'It's okay,' Lily says, shifting her weight awkwardly. 'I came to find you because we've just got some news.'

'What is it?'

'Daniella sent us a message.'

Mia feels the concrete give out from under her. She would ask Lily to stop talking, tell her she doesn't want to hear it, but she's falling so fast she can't speak, a rush of blood in her head like a wind. She turns towards Lily, who won't meet her eyes, telling her everything she needs to know.

'Kadeja and the others never arrived at the meeting spot.'

'Are you sure?'

'We're still waiting for confirmation, but it seems that they might have been caught on the way there.'

Mia rubs her eyes again, wishing this was a bad dream. 'How do you know that?'

'It wouldn't take them more than two hours to drive three miles, even if they had to make a detour.' Lily shakes her head in resignation.

Mia wishes she could really sink into the concrete, safe in the silent cast of stone. She stares up at the bruised sky and blinks back tears. When her vision clears again, she's all alone.

* * *

'Thank you for your work,' her supervisor says and hangs up, leaving Lily alone on a deserted street. The wind is starting to pick up, playing with her hair, charging her with a heightened anxiety. She dials another number.

'Lily,' Joel says on the phone. His voice is softer than she remembers it, although it's only been ten days since they last saw each other. In the house, she moves through time as though it were water, its heaviness making her impossibly light. As much as she can, she chooses not to think of the things she's left behind, because nothing is ever really left behind. Joel's face is already starting to fray around the edges. Maybe it never was that well-defined in her mind, more an idea than a person, an instrument of protection; or perhaps that is the lie of convenience she tells herself. No need to overthink now. She knows the right thing to say. 'I've missed you.'

'Is everything okay? Are you safe?'

'Yes. I think I'll be home soon.'

'I'm glad to hear that.'

She knows the right words to say in this moment too, but her body rejects them. Even though she fails her cue, Joel picks it up, a surprisingly reliable stage whisperer: 'I love you.'

Lily swallows. She tries to replicate the phrase, but her mouth fails to form the shape of them. She hangs up and walks up the street, back into the house with the boarded windows. At once, it is a refuge and a haunted house, with so many souls trapped inside the shelter of its walls. Now that the close of Lily's assignment draws nearer, she feels reluctant to leave, a conjurer bound by her own spell.

'Where have you been?' Alice asks when she enters the kitchen.

'I went on a little walk.'

'In the storm?'

'I felt so restless.'

'Just stay inside now. It's not safe on the street.'

'Do you think it's safe here?' Lily can't help but ask.

'What do you mean?' Alice seems surprised.

'Don't you think they know about this house?'

'I was just talking about the weather.'

'Of course.'

Lily gets halfway through preparing dinner when the power cuts out. Once her eyes get used to the darkness, she ventures out of the kitchen, looking for Mia. She walks through the whispers in the living room, unable to make out a single word the guests are saying. She wonders if they are cursing her under their breath, feels their eyes on her. The whole house seems to be holding its breath in indignation. She tells herself it's just a trick of the imagination and climbs the ladder into the attic.

Lily recognises the shape inside the blanket immediately; she believes she would, even if the other people usually sharing the attic space weren't gone. She calls out her name, but there is no answer. She walks over to the shape and lays her hand on top of it, a weight she hopes brings some comfort. 'Are you asleep?'

'No,' Mia says in a small voice. 'I just don't know what else to do.'

'It's okay. You don't have to do anything.'

Lily lies down beside her, breathing in the darkness. When she closes her eyes, the screaming wind swells a tide inside her, rising high and ominous. She has never known it before, but inside her is an infinite sea, a placeless place of drowning. It is not only frightening to realise she has carried it always, but soothing also. She lets the tide surge through her, wash her clean of everything, empty the debris out of her. When she licks her lips they taste of salt.

'We don't have enough of anything,' Mia whispers, muffled by the blanket. Although her words are pragmatic, Lily can feel that they are intended as a prayer. If only they made their case well enough, maybe God would take pity on them? 'Even without the storm, things were looking bad, and now we have no guarantee that the power will be switched on again, that the scavengers will come, that we won't just starve to death in this house or drown in the gutter like rats...' her voice trails off into the damp silence. Lily pulls the blanket down just a couple of inches, just enough to plant a small kiss on Mia's sweaty forehead. She goes on to kiss her eyelids, once and then again for good measure. She wonders if there is a sea inside Mia as well, and if it is a calm one.

'What if it will be okay?' Lily says. 'What if?'

'You don't know that,' Mia says, more of a whimper than a string of words.

'I know that death is a strange thing. Sometimes it doesn't come to you even if you try very hard to seduce it, other times it strikes like lightning. It is not a problem to be solved by thinking.'

'Come on. You can't deny that this is a dangerous situation.'

'I'm not denying that. I am just saying you shouldn't think about death too much.'

'What if living is even worse?'

Lily hates that she doesn't have an immediate answer, that she allows the words to knock the wind out of her. Asking Mia to resign herself to misery is the last thing she wants to do, and the only thing her wordlessness can convey. Mia makes a wounded sound, and it feels like twisting the knife, and at the same time Lily feels so unbelievably selfish, making Mia's pain about her. Even if failing to protect Mia is all she's ever done, it's not like Mia is trying to prove that point. All Lily wants is to sink deeper into her sea, but she tries reaching through the choppy surface one more time, turning towards Mia to embrace her – lightly, lightly, careful to not place any of her real weight on her. Mia inches closer to the touch, unafraid, letting her face rest on Lily's chest.

Suddenly Lily remembers something Mia said when they were just kids – 'I wonder if souls are measured in heartbeats ... I wish I could build a codex of my soul and transmit it to outer space.' It had been a silly, passing thought, but it strikes Lily with a sudden fear. What if Mia, listening to her heart with its horrible hysterias, can tell that there is something wrong with her soul? That it's still the same flawed soul she had when she was younger? Or perhaps it has withered even more, rotten to the consistency of an overripe plum crushed underfoot, inviting evil deeds like fruit flies. Mia doesn't say a thing.

'I'm glad I'm alive,' Lily whispers, mostly as a reminder to herself. It's the only thing she knows, and she's in no rush to find out if existence can get even worse. 'And I'm glad I'm with you here. We'll get through it.' She's not quite sure what *it* is – this storm, this power outage, this summer of violence, this mass extinction event? She doesn't need certainty to have faith, not in any particular divinity, but in life itself.

For a split second, her brain floods with the vision of two bodies burning, a discoloured sunset, and she wonders if possessing the lives of other people has made her more powerful, or less. In the book she burned, there were endless poems about dying and none about killing, and suddenly Lily is overcome with the desire to confess everything, the way the blood stuck to her skin, the way the smell of charred flesh seeped into her underwear and earned her the respect of other sinners.

Her mind goes blank when Mia lifts her head and rises on her elbows, bringing her face closer to Lily's, kissing her. Lily pushes her away, not ungently. 'You're shaken,' she says. 'I don't want to take advantage of you.' It's true that she started it, kind of, but she only meant her kisses as chaste gestures of affection.

Mia seems to take that as a challenge, kissing Lily with more urgency. 'I want this,' she says in a low voice.

Lily shakes her head, feeling impossible, and does nothing to stop Mia. The closer their bodies are, the further away Mia seems to drift from her, but she doesn't think the feeling is mutual. Mia is gasping like a drowning girl, holding onto Lily so tightly, and Lily needs to tell her she is an anchor not a life raft, but how could she turn down this unspent desire? If this were a fairy tale, perhaps the kiss would have the power of transformation, although Lily has nothing better to revert to. Perhaps she could truly become Katie, at least, baking bread with no blood in her hands. Mia's fingers are so soft, and her body is so warm, and the smell of her sweat makes Lily feel like she's home. The sounds Mia makes while kissing her are happy, as though this is enough to reenchant her with the world, at least for a moment. Afraid of breaking the spell, Lily responds by yielding to the small vibrations of Mia's body, and of course she would be lying to herself if she pretended she didn't enjoy it. There is a sword hanging over her head, but it's easy enough to forget about it when Mia's hands are tangling in her hair.

If only they can get close enough to each other, maybe this moment can become a seam between them, melding them together for good. She knows Mia is trying to forget too, in fact that is the only reason this is happening. She can smell the desperation in both of their sweat, hear Mia's cries turning more broken. They start kissing again, breathing unevenly into each other's mouths, and Lily notices her face is soaked with Mia's tears.

She feels stupid for thinking she could make all the death between them disappear. If anything, it feels heavier than before, festering in the heat of their bodies. There is nothing to say. Lily gently pulls Mia's head into her lap and strokes her fingers through her ink-black hair, unwashed but still soft. Lily wishes she could repeat this simple movement for eternity. Gradually, the sad hitch disappears from Mia's breathing, and her exhalations turn softer and slower. When she drifts off to sleep, Lily feels a deep sense of relief. They don't have to put this mistake into words, at least not yet.

Lily slips out of the sleep-loosened embrace and tiptoes downstairs to see what the others are doing. As soon as she gets down the ladder, she is alarmed by the reek of despair that fills the house like a miasma. The other people in the house have gathered in the living room, some of them huddled together, others isolating themselves by the walls and corners. Alice is talking to Annie and Isobel, gesturing broadly. 'I don't want to give into it. I just don't see how we can – oh, Katie, there you are. Were you in the attic with Mia?'

Lily nods. 'She's not feeling great.'

Annie smiles humourlessly. 'Well, all of us here are having the best time of our lives, so I don't know what's wrong with her.'

Lily knows platitudes would not be appreciated, and is grateful she doesn't have to come up with one. 'I'll fetch us something to eat.'

'What do we have left?' Alice asks.

'I'll go check.'

Looking at the faces of the others, Lily isn't quite sure why they're all drained of hope now. Sure, the storm is severe, rattling the windows and flooding the streets outside – she doesn't have to glimpse through the door to know that – but it won't last forever. They've got through many other storms. She supposes they're simply exhausted, watching one disaster hit after the other. In the kitchen, someone has lit a candle on the stove, illuminating the mostly empty cupboards. There is enough flour for bread, but no electricity to bake it. One shelf is lined with cans of beans and a few tins of fish. Under the sink, Lily finds some biscuits and bags of sugar. That is enough to keep them going for a couple of days.

'Have you received any more news?' she asks the others later, carrying a tray of food into the dining room. Alice shakes her head. 'We are still waiting.'

They eat in silence, swallowing the oily fish and the dry biscuits without water. After dinner, Annie and Alice go out into the garden to collect a bucketful of rain, enough to drown out the staleness of the bread. Lily takes a small glass and a plate of food upstairs to Mia, who drinks the water but refuses to touch any-thing else. Lily is not surprised that she lacks appetite after spending most of the day lying in a daze. 'Any news?' she asks, and Lily repeats Alice's gesture.

'Nothing is happening now, except for the storm.'

'I'm dreading having to hear it.'

Lily sighs. 'Try not to think about it.'

Mia sits up on her mattress, her eyes suddenly wide with worry. 'I'm sorry if I crossed a line earlier.'

'You didn't,' Lily says. 'I liked it.'

'I wouldn't usually do something like that. I was feeling so overwhelmed by everything.' Mia pauses for a second, searching for words. 'Sometimes when I see you, my memory plays tricks on me.'

'What do you mean?'

'I look at you and I think you're someone I used to know. More than that, someone I used to love, if that is the right word. Still, I know it's unfair to impose that on you – in fact, it's insane. I should never have let myself go that far.'

'I don't mind,' Lily says, trying to put a reassuring smile on her face, even though her chest aches with a strange mixture of relief and rejection. She wishes there was something else she could say, anything, but the bitter truth of her sins and the sweet falsehood of innocuous love are equally unpalatable at this moment. All she really knows is that she cannot stand the thought of losing Mia again. She lies down beside Mia, and they spend the rest of the evening with their limbs intertwined, not kissing, the fever of desire broken into a more familiar warmth.

* * *

Like all storms before, this one passes, and the house wakes from its miserable slumber. After four days of emptying dwindling tins onto greedy plates, seeing the electricity come back on again feels like a small miracle.

'To be honest, I wasn't sure if we would be getting connected to the grid again,' Annie says. 'I remember the stuff you said, about being told to shut *certain people* out of the grid. I'm pretty sure they know about the house by now. I'm not saying I'm grateful, but it's odd that they're still allowing Alice to keep her contract.'

Mia nods emphatically, her mouth full of warm bread. She wipes her mouth with the back of her hand and says: 'I don't know. I wouldn't be surprised if those people are simply incompetent.'

There are birds singing outside, sun rays scattering through the new hole in the window glass. How quickly the soul can leap from the shadow of death. Mia can feel the scar tissue growing over this latest wound, the void left by Kadeja.

That evening they get several visitors, most of them pleasant. Mia hears an engine being turned off just outside, and it gives her a jolt of fear, but she sees Alice stepping into the yard to greet the couple stepping out of a truck. They are older, probably around Alice's age, wearing a patchwork dress and dungarees. Mia watches from the window as they all embrace and beam smiles at each other. Such a display of joy is a shock to her system. She sees Chandra and her baby join them. The other remaining guests spill out of the house after them, carrying their belongings in diminutive bags and suitcases. The couple unload a large crate from the back of the truck and start piling the luggage in. Mia runs into the yard to say goodbye, and is soon joined by Annie, Altaf and Isobel, all with equally bewildered expressions on their faces.

'I wasn't aware that our guests are leaving today,' Altaf says to Alice.

'It was a last-minute plan,' Alice explains. 'For once, everything aligned perfectly. They will be safe at my friends' farm outside the city. There is water, food, electricity, everything. As long as they get through the highway toll undetected – my friends have installed a false floor for that.'

'By the grace of God,' Altaf murmurs.

Being surrounded by smiling faces, hugs and awkward but earnest handshakes, Mia feels as though she has entered another life. She worries that they're making too much noise, attracting attention from the wrong kind of neighbours, but her anxiety is defeated by the sheer happiness radiating from the people around her.

'Thank you for everything,' Chandra says before climbing into the passenger's seat with the baby in her lap.

After the truck has vanished from sight, the organisers inspect the crate left for them. Opening it fills Mia with the same kind of excitement she once felt when she saw Ms. Davis at the foster house emptying shopping bags like giant candy wrappers, filling the shelves of the cavernous kitchen with juice boxes, sachets of hot chocolate, giant boxes of honey-golden cereal, unripe bananas. It's funny how Mia still remembers the taste of all of those things, even though she hasn't had most of them in years.

Often, it is enough simply to imagine. After knowing something once, she can keep it forever, just like the sight of golden hair or a silver blade in the sun, a glimmer of hope cutting through the grime. Sometimes she finds herself transported, almost randomly, to some place from her past. She'll be standing in the garden, or looking through the shutters, or simply lying on her mattress at night, and suddenly she remembers another place, except it doesn't feel like remembering – her mind just throws some other place at her, flooding her senses with it, and usually it makes her heart break in a quiet way. The streets leading down to the sea on the first day of the summer holiday, her new hand-me-down shoes pinching her painted toes painfully. A lemon yellow sundress. A boy walking up to her and placing his hand on her left breast, a warning. A blue ice cream cone dropping head first on sizzling concrete. The warm blood and the goodbye kiss she failed to understand. The square around the university library filled with fallen cherry blossoms, a massacre of petals. The goodbye kiss. The goodbye kiss. Shivering in her bed in the winter, feeling as though she has all the time in the world, nothing yet ruined. Bare feet on cold flooring. Ms. Davis's broad back turned to her, humming hymns over the radio.

All of it is so normal, and Mia can't take it, that these things happened to her once, and never will again. The unforgiving banality of life. She thinks she has always been more aware of it than most people, mourning for things even as they happen. Once she thought she had a revelation that this visceral yearning would be cured if only her mother would take her into her arms and cradle her for so long that she'd feel totally safe and suffocated and desperate to get away, and in her weakest moments she still believes this; but she knows it is a fantasy, a hurtful fantasy, because she doesn't just want her mother. She is greedy and wants to keep *everything all the time*, and there is surely no cure for this affliction.

Mia takes a quick look at the crate outside, and her heart swells with simple joy at what she sees – a dozen eggs, a paper bag filled to the brim with damson plums, sticky-sweet cherries, a large glass jar filled with honey. It is a small blue wunderkammer of things she's forgotten even exist.

'Leaving the city does not seem like a bad idea,' Altaf says, helping her carry the heaving crate into the kitchen. 'Alice, don't you think it might be better for us to join them?'

'Our most important task is to stay here for those left behind,' Alice says 'But I'm not forcing anyone to remain here. You're free to go if you like.'

'I'm only going if you're going,' Altaf says. Both of them laugh, but Mia can feel some tension sticking between them, Alice's lingering defensiveness about staying closer to the fire. She's sure all of them have thought about leaving, but life in the countryside cannot be all milk and honey either. Outside harvest season, Mia imagines it to be much less sweet, and she knows quiet places aren't necessarily spared the violence.

Mia has noticed that the influx of people has slowed recently; they barely get one person a week looking for shelter or to find somewhere else they could go, somewhere they thought London would be, or used to be. She doesn't want to overthink the possible reasons. She can only hope the guests they have sent to the countryside are safe and – although she is aware that is a lot to ask for – even happy. Suddenly the Prime Minister's words from some radio broadcast ring in her head, *they will be sent down to the continent*. She knew then and she knows now that those words are empty, a promise of violence, but the echo of that memory makes her wonder if there is anywhere better. Her own blessings aren't too small to be counted either. In some ways, she feels like a lucky girl, in any case luckier than her parents. For every person who made it here, into an existence of rusted tins and hunger pangs, a city lashed with the thunder of death rattles, how many lie in watery graves, inside bone-dry houses, or by some nameless roadside? If someone burned all those bodies, how many minutes of light would they make? Mia feels a lump in her throat, disturbed by her own thoughts.

'Are you alright?' Annie asks her, holding out a plate of scones slathered with strawberry jam.

'Yes,' she says and bites into a scone. The density of flavour is overwhelming. She doesn't want to talk about the way she feels, or anything at all. Alice leaves the dining room and returns with Nick, who greets them all in his subdued way. Mia always finds his presence to be calming, although she supposes that is a knack of double agents, to make others feel at ease in the presence of real threats. 'I have bad news,' he says, to nobody's surprise. 'The activists who have been arrested so far have been systematically tortured for information, and most of them have been killed. I didn't even have to dig around – they could bear to be a lot more discreet about it.'

Mia has already practised this scene in her head over and over again, but the rehearsals hurt far less than this.

'Do you know if Jamie and Kadeja are still alive?' Alice asks, and Mia is grateful for this, because she would've been too much of a coward to do anything but delay the inevitable.

Nick shakes his head. 'I haven't seen them, nor any paperwork related to them, but I would advise against being overly hopeful.'

'Of course.'

They stand around awkwardly, unsure how to proceed to any other topic when there is barely any air left in the room. 'Would you like some –' Alice says, vaguely gesturing towards the food laid out on the table.

'That looks beautiful,' Nick says. 'Where did you get it from?'

'Biggin Hill,' Alice says. 'My old friends there have been very good to us this year.'

'Have you considered packing up and moving there, or somewhere else outside the city? I could help arrange safe transport for you. I fear it's a question of time until you become a direct target.'

'I understand what you're saying, but our most important work is here – so many people are struggling to get by in the city, there has to be some sort of a network to support them, or at least contact points to help them leave. They have kindly taken in several of our guests this summer.'

While she speaks, Nick's attention strays elsewhere. Lily enters the room with a jug full of water, and Nick immediately turns towards her. Through her haze of grief, Mia watches them react to each other in a strange manner, both of their mouths opening as though something is just on the tip of their tongues. Nick seems to cull the impulse by biting into an egg sandwich. Lily sets the jug down on the table with a clang, inhaling so hard Mia can see her lungs move through her shirt. There is no doubt in Mia's mind that they know each other; not only that, there is some bad blood between them, making the atmosphere of the room feel even more oppressive. She is desperate to know more, but their clear reluctance to talk about it leaves no room for her to voice any questions.

Nick finishes his bread quickly and refuses dessert. 'I'll just use your outhouse, and then I'll be on my way,' he says. 'Again, I am sorry to always be a bearer of bad news.' Mia watches Lily leave the room soon after him. She stays inside, trying to remain present in the conversations other people are having, but the urge to find out what's going on proves irresistible. She follows the trail of faint voices towards the muddy garden, standing behind the door to avoid being found out. Eavesdropping makes her face burn with embarrassment, but it's too late to stop now.

'It's not like that. I haven't told them anything.'

Lily's voice sounds harsher and lower than usual. Maybe it's because it's being filtered through the door, or maybe they're having an argument – she can't tell, just yet.

'If you do that, I'll have nowhere to go.'

Her tone turns more pleading. Nick says something in return, but so softly Mia can't make out his words. They keep bickering like that for a while, and Mia becomes more and more certain that there is some history of heartbreak between them – maybe Nick doesn't want Lily to expose details of his other life? – until Nick finally raises his voice enough for Mia to hear every word.

'You can make all the promises in the world, Lily, but if you can't prove that you're not the one who leaked the plans last week, how am I supposed to trust you? Several people could be dead because of you.'

Suddenly everything makes so much sense that none of it does, the architecture of Mia's daily reality shifting around her so rapidly she can barely stay upright. She stumbles into the kitchen and starts wiping the stacks of dishes someone has brought in from lunch.

The worst thing is not being sure if she knew, from the moment she first saw her in that meeting weeks ago, that the truth was likely to be something far worse than she wanted it to be. You can make yourself believe anything. She has been breathing in clues like air, starting from Lily's inexplicable reluctance to acknowledge everything they had shared before, the veneer of nonchalant cooperativeness so at odds with her usual intensity. Her odd bursts of violence, much less bloody and pronounced now than in their childhood, but still – she should've read her fortune in the charred ashes of whatever Lily burned in the middle of the night, meeting Mia's eyes with that horrible blade-glint gaze. Just a couple of days after that odd ritual, Lily must have set the trap for Kadeja to walk into. It's all so much uglier than she can bear, and her mind keeps replaying the kisses they exchanged in dizzying detail. It's not the kind of thing Mia would usually do. She's always been best at pushing people away, keeping them at arm's length even when she knows affection would win them over. She knows now why it felt so easy to make an exception. Now the weight of Lily's sins is upon her, and she doesn't think she knows even half of it. The muddier their environment, the more pure and beautiful lilies are supposed to grow, but even their petals must get stained in a lake of blood.

Mia has stood there, wiping figures of eight on the same dish with a dirty rag for at least a quarter of an hour, when Lily enters the kitchen.

'I can do the dishes,' she says, and Mia hears her taking a step forward. It makes her stomach turn.

'Stay away,' she says, and Lily doesn't push it, standing very still in the middle of the kitchen. 'What's going on?' she asks, and Mia wonders if the confusion in her voice is feigned.

'I don't think I need to spell it out to you.' She wants to say Lily's name, spit it out for dramatic effect, but the word feels so ruined in her mouth now that she'd rather throw up battery acid. Lily makes a small wounded sound, and Mia sees this as an opening to stick her knife in. 'I heard Nick call your name. Is he an old friend from the office?'

She still can't bring herself to say it. As long as she doesn't say it, maybe there is still a sliver of a chance that this is a misunderstanding, that she didn't hear correctly, that she has simply gone mad. The fortnight they have spent together in the house has been more pleasant than it really should have been, all things considered. For a brief moment, she could see the grief-clouded horizon shed itself and rise again in watercolour blue, a lonely dazzling dream. Lily doesn't have to say anything; the curtains have already closed on that world. Mia still wants more answers, but the scale of her questions paralyses her. She starts from what is closest at hand.

'I knew from the start it was you,' Mia says. 'I knew from the start.'

Lily only looks surprised for the blink of an eye. She must have rehearsed this many times before. 'I was hoping you would. That you hadn't forgotten me.'

'I was just waiting for you to tell me why.'

'I wanted to tell you. It's not easy.'

Mia takes a deep breath and places her hand down on the kitchen counter, but it doesn't do much to ground her. She feels drunk with dread, the air within the room moving in waves around her. 'What exactly is it that you wanted to tell me?'

'You know my real name. You know everything there really is to know about me.'

'Is that so? It seems to me that something must have changed. Why did you try to hide your identity?' Mia is satisfied to see the flicker of fear in Lily's eyes. She knows she's really getting to her, at last. She keeps staring at Lily, daring her to say something, until the silence grows deadly. 'You're working for the Party, aren't you? You told them to arrest Kadeja and the others. I heard you in the garden.'

'It's not that simple,' Lily protests quietly.

'But you're not denying it?'

'It's not that I wanted to do it, any of it – it's been painful for me too.'

'Oh, fuck off.' Mia moves from grief to rage so quickly she sees Lily shiver. 'You have no right to even speak about pain.'

'I'm sorry,' Lily says, but Mia just waves her hand angrily.

'Surely you understand that this is not something that can ever be forgiven?'

Lily shakes her head slightly, her eyes gleaming in the lamplight. Mia doesn't want to think about how many hours of her life she has wasted hoping to find Lily again, to be found by her; long enough that tears of shame fall from her eyes. 'You were the only person I've ever really felt loved by, maybe the only person I've really loved. I know we were just kids, but still. You've never stopped hurting me.'

Lily looks straight at her, mouth agape, but it seems she can't find the words she is looking for.

'I was the only person at Buckley Street to get a scholarship, you know,' Mia says, to drive in the difference between them, although the words sound terribly flimsy and self-aggrandising as soon as they leave her mouth. 'I worked hard and got a good degree. I was desperate to pay it all forward. What did you do after running away? Got bored of living on the street so you decided to become a fascist rat instead?'

'That's not true.'

'Really? That's how it seems to me.'

'You don't know that much about me.'

'I know you're the reason nobody has killed us in our beds yet, right? You're fattening us up until the moment we're no longer useful enough to be kept alive.' Mia can feel her voice rising to a level it has not reached in years, maybe ever, and the force of it almost scares her. 'You broke the generator, didn't you?'

'I was trying to protect you.'

The words feel like a slap in the face, and Mia can barely contain a scream lodged in her throat. 'You cannot protect me by killing my friends.'

'I look at you and I feel something I didn't know I still could.' Lily wrenches her hands. 'There must be a reason we met like this. I've never really known what I am living for, but when I'm with you, all I want to do is to protect you.'

Mia shakes her head. 'No. If you wanted to protect us, you could have told us from the start, arranged an exit route, done anything other than *this*.'

'I've worked so hard to build a better life for myself. If I threw it all away, what would I have?' Lily pleads.

Maybe you could have had another chance of sharing your life with me, your real life, your real self, Mia thinks, but she cannot bring herself to say those words out loud.

'I can still get you out of here,' Lily continues, more frantically. 'I'll vouch for you. I can get you a job, a steady job, a flat with running water – a future.'

'Don't insult me like that,' Mia says. 'I am not free to think only about myself.'

'Of course you're worried about everyone else in this house. But can't you see you're all doomed?'

'Shut up,' Mia shouts, louder than she knew she had the capacity for. 'The people you've murdered mean the world to me. You're nothing compared to them.'

'I'm the only one that can help you.'

'You come here, destroy everything, and then nominate yourself as some kind of saviour. ' Mia takes a step towards Lily and shoves her against the wall. 'I wish I'd never met you. You've always been nothing but bad news.'

She grabs Lily's face and presses on her jaw hard enough to bruise. Lily does nothing to fight back, falling still beneath her hands. 'I hate you so much,' Mia hisses and moves her hand to Lily's throat, pushing down on her pulse. Their eyes meet while she's strangling her, and the look in Lily's eyes is so pitiful it makes her want to throw up. She withdraws her hand as though it's been burned and catches her breath, still reeling from her sudden outburst. Still leaning against the wall, Lily raises her hands in a gesture of surrender. 'If you hate me so much, why don't you just kill me and run with your friends? You can be free. I'll help you get away with it. You can strangle me, stab me, burn me to death, anything your heart desires.'

Mia can't tell whether this is supposed to be a joke, a dare, or a serious plea. There is a glint of arrogance in Lily's eyes that Mia really can't stand, as though she's still convinced she knows better. Her whole body is shaking with anger, and the flashes of it frighten her with their intensity. She has never felt this urge before, telling her to hurt and maim. Her fingers find the handle of a knife on the kitchen counter, and the weight of the sharp object is calming. This must be fate. When she takes a step forward, Lily closes her eyes and goes stone still. Mia can hear her younger voice in her ears, telling her to stop being such a coward, to start protecting herself. There is another voice, one she doesn't quite recognise, telling her that hurting Lily will not be enough, chopping her into a thousand pieces will not be enough. Lily's face is taut, eyes squeezed shut, arms hanging stiffly by her sides. Mia's hand hovers far away from the soft parts Lily has exposed, refusing to draw closer. The shaking is getting worse. Adrenaline surges through her veins, but despite the thousand alarms going off in her body, she can't move further than this. What a show of weakness; something has to break!

'Please,' Lily whispers, and Mia doesn't think she's asking her to stop. She always did have a strange obsession with being hurt, wearing her various bruises and cuts with misplaced pride, even asking Mia to make them worse. 'Please,' she repeats. It's all too much; Mia can't give her the satisfaction. Lily opens her eyes, and her expression is strange, unreadable, as though she is not seeing Mia at all. In the face of apparent indifference, a shiver runs through Mia, a cold fear that the girl she once loved is long dead. This could still be revenge, twice bitten, thirsty for blood, she thinks in that split second. Lily might believe herself to be so above it all, like nothing ever touches her, but Mia knows the sight of her slashing her own wrist would be burnt onto her retinas forever, a fitting punishment. The blade presses against the soft skin beside her wrist like a firm caress, quickly growing bolder with bloodlust. There is a wet scrape, a scream of colour, Lily shouting words that make no sense. The knife shakes in Mia's sticky grip, and Lily closes the distance they have kept so far, taking it away from her with dexterity. Mia's heart skips a beat when the bleeding starts, and every subsequent throb is an exclamation mark, her whole body seized with an alarming clarity of not wanting to die. The worst of the pain hits her with a five-second delay, pushing her off the verge of tears, but at least she has succeeded in taking Lily down with her. Lily is touching her weakly, weeping while she tries to inspect the wound and, even despite all the pain, Mia's heart is soothed by a sense of vindication. She can see Lily's lips forming words, but the rush of blood in her ears has grown too loud to make them out.

Suddenly Nick is there, taking the knife from Lily's hands – she parts with it easily, a cursed object – while Alice's hands cradle Mia's slippery wrist, trying to push the life back inside her. She sees Annie and Altaf rushing into the room and grab Lily's arms to hold her still. Although Lily does nothing to physically resist, an argument develops between the three of them. There is a lot of shouting, but everything is filtered through a thick fog. Mia sees Annie's face hovering over her, brows knitted in concern, just before the floor slips away underneath her and she falls into a strange restless slumber.

A burning sting, almost more painful than the initial bite of the blade, wakes her up. 'Thank God, it's not as bad as it looks,' Alice whispers, cleaning the wound. Mia looks away, her eyes skimming over the spines of dusty books she has not read crammed into the bookshelves of the storage room. She is propped up on a large cardboard box, her hand on Alice's shoulder. Alice tells her it's

going to be alright, although Mia doesn't think she really understands the situation at all; neither does she, free-falling as she is.
Alice murmurs other reassuring things. If Mia closes her eyes, she
can almost imagine it's her mother, the kinds of words a mother
would say. She realises she has never even asked if Alice has children, and the gulf between her and other people feels so impossibly
wide, as though she has never known a single reliable thing about
another person.

'I'm sorry,' Mia says, as Alice wraps a thick cuff of gauze
around her wrist. 'I didn't mean to cause so much trouble.'

'I'm sorry. We should have noticed sooner that something was
going on.'

Mia shakes her head. 'It's not your fault. I think I knew the
whole time.' Her heart contracts painfully.

'Why didn't you tell us?'

The words sound damning to Mia, but Alice's tone is gentle.
She leans back against the wall, considering the truth. It is not
easy to think lucidly about it. 'I hoped that as long as I didn't say
it, it might not be true.' Her body feels so cold her teeth are starting to chatter.

'And you didn't want it to be true,' Alice says, a
half-question.

Mia shakes her head. She touches her face with her uninjured
hand and feels it is slick with saltwater. She is afraid of what she
might say, and then the words come out horribly loud, exclam-
ations of anguish. 'I could never stop loving her. Maybe I still can't.
I can't stand the thought of losing her even if having her means
losing everything else.' Her voice is getting choked up, and she
stops to catch her breath, but it's too late to keep her silence now.
'I told Kadeja to trust her, even when I should have known what
she was. Her blood is on my hands.'

'You didn't kill anyone,' Alice says sternly.

'I might as well have.' Mia is shaking all over, remembering the way Lily's arms felt around her, the taste of her mouth when they kissed, all while Kadeja was falling into her trap. Mia wipes her lips with the back of her hand and glances at Alice fearfully, expecting her to raise her voice. Instead, Alice wraps her arms around her ribcage, holding her just tightly enough to make her feel contained. At first, Mia wants to resist the embrace – it is more gentleness than she can take – but she forces herself to stay. They stay like that for a long time. Alice gives away enough warmth to stop Mia's shaking completely, but despite her physical stillness, Mia is falling through a kaleidoscope of emotions all tinged with an almost unbearable sense of shame. 'I should have just done it,' she mutters into Alice's shirt, holding her bandaged wrist with her uninjured hand.

'What do you mean?' Alice asks, her hand drawing circles on Mia's back, little spells that fail to soothe her. Mia can't bring herself to say it, but the conviction weighs on her like a bag of stones, and she knows Alice can feel it too. No matter how badly Mia might have been hurt, she was a willing participant, content to lead her kin to slaughter.

'I used to think she was my guardian angel. I always knew she had the capacity for violence, but I thought she would only use it to protect me – I was so fucking delusional – I've never wanted anyone like I wanted her. She is a monster, and so am I. I sacrificed Kadeja for her.' For some reason, Alice keeps holding her even as she cries and curses, admits things nobody should ever know, things that should disqualify her from anyone's kindness.

'I don't deserve to be here,' she whispers, and of course Alice voices her disagreement, but it's only a formality. Both of them know the truth. Finally, it feels as though all words are emptied out of her, crystallised into a bloodied lump of sadness and anger in her core. She knows she must carry it within her for the rest of her life.

By the time they emerge from the storage room, the house has gone dark and quiet around them. Mia wonders if everyone heard the things she and Lily screamed at each other in the kitchen, her shameful confession to Alice. The others have as much reason to hate her as they do Lily. Her reassurance to Kadeja keeps replaying in her head – 'I would trust her with my life, please let her stay' – mocking her so cruelly she wants to hit her skull against a wall just to stop listening.

The first thing Mia notices after entering the room is that Lily is seated at the table, her head in her hands, while Nick and Annie and Altaf all glower around her. Their faces lighten ever so slightly at the sight of Mia alive and relatively unscathed, but Mia barely notices, her whole being singularly focused on the offending presence. She almost turns around and runs out of the door, but her body freezes up.

'You should have kicked her out,' she says under her breath, even if a part of her is relieved to see Lily, the part she knows she must seal off forever.

'That is the plan,' Nick says, picking up on her quiet cursing. 'We are just trying to decide *how*.'

'Most importantly, are you okay?' Annie asks, and Mia nods before deciding against it, shaking her head instead. 'I don't know. My wrist is fine. I'm sorry for making you worry.'

'Don't apologise.'

'Are you going to kill her?' Mia asks, taking care not to look in Lily's direction. It feels strange, to say those words so casually, as though she was talking about a chicken in the yard instead of someone she thought she would be bonded to forever. It feels callous, and necessary.

'We would rather avoid it,' Altaf says. 'But it is an option we must consider.'

'She said we should either kill her or let her work on our side,' Annie says with a wry smile. 'She promised she'd honour her word this time.'

'So considerate,' Altaf says.

'We have to get rid of her one way or another,' Annie says, sighing. 'I can't stand to look at her for another five minutes.'

Lily remains silent, staring down at her lap.

'We were waiting for you, Mia,' Nick says, holding her gaze. 'I think you deserve the last word on this. You know her better than the rest of us.'

Mia wants to scoff at that, to deny that she's ever known Lily at all – or to point out that she is an accomplice and should be punished alongside her. Still, it seems unwise to argue instead of finding a solution. Slowly, Mia turns to look at her old friend, and Lily meets her eyes. She looks worse for wear, her face mottled with fresh bruises and welts, and her hands tied to the chair behind her back. Nevertheless, there is the familiar wilfulness in her eyes, the righteousness that pushed Mia off the edge before.

'Don't say anything,' she says. 'There are things I need to say to you.' There is no response.

'I never want to see you again,' she begins, and Lily looks as though she's been struck in the face anew. Mia realises this whole time she must have been holding on to a perverse hope of an everlasting bond between them; that is why she'd ask for death before being discarded. Mia can almost hear the wheels turning in Lily's head, trying to come up with one more reason to stay, but everyone in the room knows there are no moves left in this game.

Mia wonders if Lily's heart ever stops changing, if there is anything in this world that will keep her from straying off the paths she once chose. Perhaps if everything was different, it would not need to be so serious. Lily could keep running in circles around the people she loves, change direction and turn around when the wind changes, indulge in her fickleness. They could cross paths every now and then, touch each other lightly. If only everything was different. In the present, Mia must acknowledge the part of her that still craves Lily's proximity only so she can deny it with all her might.

'Maybe it makes me a coward, but I couldn't stand burying you,' she concedes. 'Even so, you owe us your life.'

'What do you want me to do with it?' Lily looks up at Mia with a feverish glint in her eyes. 'I'm not asking for your forgiveness. Just tell me what to do.'

Mia squeezes her eyes shut and rubs circles on her brows, as though easing a headache. Everyone's eyes are fixed on her, observing her every movement. She never thought she would enjoy holding someone's life in her hands, but the way Lily is finally yielding to her feels right. For once, Lily seems to have learned a lesson, even if it took Mia shedding her own blood. 'I want nothing more than to go back in time and stop you from causing so much pain, but none of it can be undone,' she says, carefully, taking a step towards Lily, 'there will be no easy absolution.'

'I'll do anything.'

'I want you to go back to your world and end it.' She bends down to caress Lily's cheek, and Lily nuzzles her hand in response, more malleable than Mia has ever seen her be. The gesture of affection embarrasses Mia, but she cannot withdraw, not if this helps them get out of this mess. 'Of course,' Lily says. 'I'll take revenge for you.'

Mia turns to the rest of the organisers. 'What should we have her do?'

'We could make it memorable. Maybe the same fireworks we had in mind for the Ministry of Water,' Annie says.

'I like the idea, but it is best to keep it simple,' Altaf responds.

'We've had so many plans fail already,' Alice agrees. 'And there is nothing to suggest Lily is an exceptionally competent agent.'

'I think it would make sense to target her office, the social affairs division' Nick says. 'If I remember correctly, the Prime Minister's niece works there. Is that true, Lily?'

'Yes. I know her quite well.'

'Losing a friend is hard,' Annie says wryly. 'But I think you're used to it by now.'

She goes to the window and lifts it half-open, craving some fresh air. The stench of sewers and floral putrefaction drifts in from the street. It is the season of decay.

'Revenge is not enough, but it's the best we can do, me and you,' Mia whispers, close to Lily's ear. She places her hand on Lily's head and strokes her hair, animated by the certainty that they will never speak again. 'I was always expecting you to leave.' The words feel knife-sharp, the steel of them rusted with so many years of silence, steeped in the ugly brown of old blood.

Celebration

ALL THE LINES Lily had practised run through her head blotchy and illegible, lines of ink washing away in the rain. What is left is a jagged black seed, hard and shiny inside her, and she doesn't know what to call it. She is frightened of whatever might grow out of it.

It's getting dark, and she has nowhere to go, now that the kindness of strangers has finally run out. She imagines the rusting lock on the front door of Joel's flat, sliding her key in like an afterthought, the room just like she left it a month ago: her work clothes folded over a kitchen chair, the folder of lies on the windowsill, the floor unswept. She sinks into it, replacing the present with the countless images of this, something like this, flowing from within her. It's not difficult at all. Joel shoving her onto the bed, tearing at fabric and skin. Some of the sensations are pleasant. A belt sliding over her throat smoothly at first, a mock caress, until it loops into a figure-eight around her neck. She hasn't tried using her voice for a while, but now she does, and it's trapped. The lights are off, but every split second births a new star; by the time he lets go, it's a galaxy. Gasping for bone-dry air, Lily feels they are already in the post-mortem. Her fingers clench in the emptiness of her skirt pocket. She must have left the keys in the house on Milkwood Road. Locked out of her old self, she keeps walking, vaguely heading towards the river.

The water is black and topped with a layer of debris like filthy seafoam. For a moment, Lily considers drowning, but she knows it's not in her. She's always been a quitter, only the reverb of past lives keeps growing louder. She wants nothing more than to run away, shed her skin and start over again, but she is imprisoned by the look of contempt in Mia's eyes. With every step, the black seed grows heavier.

It shouldn't surprise Lily when her biometric chip opens the heavy door to the Ministry of Social Affairs without a hitch. An armed security guard scans her chip a second time and finds nothing contentious about her presence. In the grey pre-dawn, the corridors are chilly and lifeless. She walks into her office, which is completely unchanged, and sits at her desk. Bone-tired after the night spent walking, pretending her destination isn't fixed, she lays her head down against the hard surface of the desk and falls into a deep slumber. The flick of the light switch wakes her up a few hours later. Joel is standing by the door, looking at her with a raised eyebrow. 'Why are you back, all of a sudden?'

'I was recalled by my supervisors,' Lily says. 'They consider the terrorist unit to be successfully defanged by now.'

'Why didn't you come home, then?'

'I don't know. I guess I felt like I needed to be alone. And I lost my keys.'

'I would have let you in, idiot. I'm glad to have you back safe.'

'Thanks. I'm relieved to be here. It was stressful.' She knows her words sound flat, almost mocking.

Joel walks to Lily and wraps his arms around her shoulders from behind. 'You got through it.'

'How have things been here?'

'Oh, the same as usual. Security level has been raised across the government, after what happened with Water and the Home

Office. But our department doesn't quite top the list of sexiest targets.'

'It must be up there, though.'

'No doubt. We are preparing for the worst.'

'Let's talk about something else,' Lily says.

'Let's not talk at all.' Joel's hands descend on Lily's hips, pulling at the hem of her underwear with a familiar hunger. She doesn't want to give in so easily, but she's too tired to argue against it. The weeks of separation have not made her heart grow any fonder towards Joel, nor her body, but neither is touching him more objectionable than it used to be. It is herself that she finds more despicable than before, not him. She feels keenly the contrast to the strange lust that burned in her when Mia gave her condemnation mere hours ago. It feels like a blessing, to remember how it is to want something with all her power, even if her desires will go unfulfilled. It bonds her to this drowning world.

Afterwards, Lily goes to her locker and checks that the knife she hid there during days of laxer security still lies hidden in the folds of her spare shirt. She straps the sheathed blade to the belt beneath her dress and wanders off to the canteen, which is just opening up for the morning. The relative abundance of things is quite startling – there are metal jugs of milk beside pots of half-and-half tea, sandwiches filled with eggs and grilled vegetables, fatty sausages and pastries with cream. She is unsure if it was always like this, or if the supply has improved recently. In the house, things could have been worse, but she got used to hunger like a minor toothache. She eats until she feels sick and then goes to the ladies' room. The mirror on the wall is large and sparklingly clean, and Lily realises she hasn't seen her reflection this clearly in a long time. The only mirror in the activists' house was scratched and dirty, and nobody ever seemed to care enough to polish it.

She's relied on the soft spectres in night-time windows to take stock of herself, and the stark angles of her face, the dark circles and the ghastly cheekbones exacerbated by the freshly blooming bruises take her by surprise. She no longer looks young. She bends down over the sink, opens the tap and splashes water all over her miserable face. Suddenly someone shrieks her name, and her body tenses up, ready to fight. She glances at the mirror and sees Amelia behind her, flashing a toothy smile. As soon as Lily turns around, she's being enveloped in a crushing hug. 'You look tired,' Amelia says, politely declining to ask about the injuries.

'I just got back from my assignment this morning.'

'How was it?'

'It was okay. I can't really talk about it, at least not before my debrief.' Lily can't decide whether she should kill Amelia now, in the relative privacy of the bathroom, or bide her time. She knows the easiest thing would be to knock Amelia unconscious, drag her into a stall and get the hell out, but that seems lacklustre. Fulfilling her promise to Mia requires making a big scene, something to remember for eternity, as they all burn in hell together.

'I understand. It's okay. I've missed you so much – the boys have been awful.'

'I bet. Why don't you ever get your aunt to do something about it?'

Amelia grimaces. 'Can't. Anyway, we should celebrate your return. Can I get you a drink?'

'This early in the morning?'

'It's not a crime.'

'Why not?' Lily says, and follows Amelia back into the office, which looks much busier at this hour. It seems there have been some personnel changes in her absence, but all of her least favourite colleagues are still there. Malcolm is standing over Joel's desk, going over some documents with the same sour expression he always wears. Lily is relieved when he makes no move to acknowledge her presence, even though Joel must have at least mentioned it. Amelia goes into the little kitchen to fetch a bottle and a number of glasses, arranging them in a neat row on Lily's table.

'What's this?' Malcolm says, finally enticed to look towards them.

'Celebrating Lily's return', Amelia says in a small voice. She still can't look him in the eye.

'Perhaps Lily can afford to drink the day away, but I don't think the same applies to you,' he says, but doesn't sound that incensed.

'I wasn't going to drink.'

'Fine, then. Feel free to pour me one.'

Lily watches Amelia fill the glasses with a steady hand. Something about the motion is dreadfully hypnotic. After she is finished with the liquor, Amelia goes to get a plastic bottle of Evian from the office fridge and pours herself some. When they're all clinking their glasses and saying platitudes Lily supposes this is as good as it will ever get.

'I heard you stopped the attack on the Ministry of Water,' Amelia says. 'I wanted to tell you I really admire you for that. I wish I could be as brave as you.'

'I wouldn't be surprised if the security people give you some type of commandment,' Malcolm says and slaps Lily on the back. 'Just mention us in your acceptance speech, please. We've always taken good care of you, haven't we?'

'Do you want her to write you a little poem for good measure?' Joel asks.

Lily downs her drink with a grimace. The thought of being bestowed with some Party accolade, a marine blue rosette and a wax-stamped letter, makes her shudder.

'I'm sorry, I need to go to the washroom,' she says and walks away from the little party. At least here she doesn't need to hide her lack of manners half as much.

It is easier to breathe when she's alone in a cubicle. She stares down at the sparkling clean toilet bowl and tries to make herself throw up, but nothing materialises except a few drops of blood. She gets up and wipes the snot off her face. The idea of shattering the mirror suddenly tempts her, but she knows that would be idiotic. She can't attract attention before going through with her grand finale. She turns away from her reflection and closes her eyes, trying to think it through.

Amelia's death would cause the greatest collateral damage, an attack on the Prime Minister's bloodline, so Lily should take her down first. Amelia has been filling in for Lily's job of reviewing travel permit applications, so she'll ask if she can review her work. She'll sit at her desk for a while, going over the documents like good old times, not really reading what's in front of her. She'll pretend to find a major problem, a high-profile Party donor whose request Amelia has rejected, and go over to her desk to confront her about it.

'I think you should check in with your aunt about this,' she'll say. 'Otherwise you might end up in trouble.' Amelia will reach out for her mobile phone and make the call, and as soon as the Prime Minister responds – if she doesn't, Lily will simply try again later, she doesn't have all the time in the world but she does have a couple of hours or days – Lily's knife will be at her throat. With the blade as her intermediary, she won't feel Amelia's pulse throbbing beneath her fingers. It will be altogether neater than the last time and, besides, she won't have to live with it for long.

There is no doubt that Amelia will scream, high and glass-bright; Lily can already picture it. She'll have no demands or requests for the Party, nothing to relay. The only thing to communicate is despair. After Amelia, she will slit as many other throats as possible before slashing her own. If her plan doesn't work out, she'll just follow her monstrous instincts.

As Lily is imagining the office drowned in blood, Amelia walks into the restroom. 'Do you feel okay?' she asks by way of greeting. 'You can take the rest of the day off if you're exhausted. I could talk to Joel.'

'I'll be okay. I need to get back into the pace of things,' Lily says, disturbed by the afterimages of the bloodletting in her mind superimposed on Amelia's friendly face. Amelia goes into a cubicle and locks the door. It feels like a cruel joke, to be alone with her in the washroom for the second time that day.

'It's hard to believe you've only been gone for a couple of weeks. So much has changed,' Amelia says through the door. When Lily does not respond, she continues: 'It seems like everyone's on their toes. The situation with the military is getting worse.'

Lily does not know much about the situation, and she's not in the mood to ask. The future seems short.

'At least it seems that Weather Underwater is less of a threat now,' Amelia says.

'It was never really a threat.'

'What do you mean? They've killed people.'

'Sure,' Lily says, turning the tap on and off. Her hand travels to her knife belt, caressing the leather sheath. Amelia comes out of the cubicle, washes her hands and arranges her hair, which looks impossibly shiny, as though she cleanses it with water and shampoo multiple times a week. 'Would you like some?' she asks, taking out a small compact of baby-pink rouge.

'No thank you,' Lily says. 'I'm still getting used to how my regular face looks.'

'Did the terrorists not have mirrors? I could never live like that.'

They walk down the corridor together, and Lily tries in vain to listen to Amelia's gossip about the new hires. The adrenaline coursing through her body is making it impossible to think about anything but the blood she is about to spill.

'Oh, by the way, Joel said you were handling my work when I was gone,' she says as they walk through the door of the office. 'Could you let me do some spot checks?'

'Of course.'

Lily returns to her desk with a thick stack of documents and sits still for a while, watching Amelia in the back of the office. Her big blue eyes are glazing over the paperwork like they always do. She takes little gulps of water and licks her lips after every one, looking endlessly sad and paradoxically powerless. Lily always thought how funny it is that those closest to power can convince themselves they have none. The charade must reach its conclusion.

Glass horizon

MIA RUNS OUT of the house and through the front garden, stopping at the threshold of the street. She sees Lily walking away, head held high, looking perfectly sure of her destination. Mia doesn't expect her to look back, and she's right. The setting sun makes Lily's hair look brighter than it really is, wheat in harvesttime. Mia feels certain she will never see Lily's face again, and that she will make her peace with it. Watching her back without calling out to her feels like a coward's goodbye, but it is not. It would be more cowardly to yield once again. Lily turns the corner and disappears.

Back in the house, Alice is standing in the hallway, talking to someone on a burner phone. 'As soon as possible,' she says as Mia walks past her into the kitchen, where Annie and Isobel are packing the few remaining items from the cupboard into a cardboard box, bags of sugar taking up the bulk of the space. 'We're leaving?' Mia asks, and Annie nods in response.

'Alice is already making arrangements.'

'That's quick.'

'We can't be quick enough. She's a psycho. She's definitely going to set someone on us.'

Despite everything, Mia feels an urge to defend Lily, to say there is still a chance she is not all rotten at heart; but she knows better than to voice it. The urge in itself is a shameful thing, another reminder that she would let a wolf through the gates just for a shred of affection. She still doesn't know if she has ever really been in love, but she has every reason to be afraid of it.

Alice walks into the kitchen, mercifully interrupting Mia's thought spiral. 'We're going to leave the city. You know how much I want to stay here, but even I have to admit it would be very foolish. Some friends are coming to get us in two hours. It doesn't matter if we don't manage to pack up everything – let's just take a few things. They have everything we really need.' Her brow furrows as she looks at Mia. 'My dear, you look like you're about to faint. Please go and lie down. I'll come get you. And I promise things will get better than this, at least.'

Although Mia hates feeling like a burden, she can't deny that being ordered to rest is a relief. She walks through the living room, and the sound of her own footsteps is startlingly loud now that the mattresses have been stacked elsewhere. Even if this house has never felt exactly like a home, it's the closest to one she's had since leaving Buckley Street. If her head weren't full of other painful things, she would probably feel wistful, climbing the ladder up to the attic for the last time.

Her own mattress and the thin duvet cover are still there, and they can stay, whether that means until someone returns or until they decompose into strands of synthetic fibres. She lies down on the mattress one last time and closes her eyes, imagining that it's night-time in April, cold and clear. Kadeja and Jamie are breathing slowly on either side of her, exuding gentle body warmth. She laces their fingers together and they clasp her hand, reaching out through the veil of sleep.

Mia's mind strays to another cold night, Lily curled up on the edge of a narrow bunk bed, teeth chattering even though she's wearing an overcoat. Her eyes are soft and watery, as though she is pleading Mia for an impossible salvation, a spectral child-self desperate to undo the future. This is how Mia wants to picture Lily, shattered with regret, but she knows it is wishful thinking. Lily will probably keep haunting her dreams forever. It doesn't matter. The ghost in her head cannot hurt those close to her.

'Mia.'

She hears Alice's voice calling her name, the soft sound of feet on ladder steps. 'We're going soon.' Alice's head emerges through the doorway. 'How are you feeling?'

'I'll be fine.'

Alice walks over to her and sits down beside the mattress. Once again, Mia feels like a patient being cared for by a nurse, or mothered, a strange word with a stranger meaning.

'There is no rush to be fine. It's important to give yourself time.'

'It's just ... it feels unreal how much things have changed in a year. Last summer, I was saying my goodbyes to the city I grew up in, preparing to travel to London, to take up a job doing something meaningful. I had no idea any of this would happen, losing so many people, feeling scared all the time. It's not like things were perfect then, but it's hard to believe how much worse they can get in a year.'

'If things can get worse, they can also get better,' Alice says quietly. 'The future is not decided.'

'I find that equally hard to believe,' Mia says bitterly.

'And I don't blame you for that. But I've been hearing promising things from outside London.'

'It feels like we're just escaping in panic.'

'That's not wrong, but it's only the start. You'll see. This world will never be perfect, but it will be better than this. And even if you're not completely fine, you'll be part of it, and you'll feel the change radiate within yourself also. You don't have to trust me, but if you keep living, you'll know what I mean.'

Alice leaves Mia to gather the things she has kept in the attic. There are not many; the weight of everything she has lost while living here must be many times greater than that of her possessions.

Downstairs, the pile of luggage is quite small. Alice has left most of the mundane objects untouched, relics of the years she spent living a normal life in this house. 'I hope I get to come back here someday,' she sighs, dragging a suitcase with one broken wheel through the door. 'I'll leave a spare key in the usual place, in case any of you need to return – although I am not sure whether this will ever be a safe house again.' She stays inside for a little longer than everyone else. Mia thinks it's no wonder she's so attached to it, what with all the life it has absorbed.

They wait in the driveway, overgrown with weeds. Mia sits on a cardboard box and stares up at the transparent blue of the afternoon sky. The whole world has a fragile glow of glass, as though it could fall apart at any second. She keeps waiting for things to change.

Through what window do you gaze and see eternity?

THE JOURNEY TO the docks is just a ripple tide. Lily watches the scenery through dark glass, another storm gathering, the sky an evil eye winking at her. It's all so beautiful before the end.

They stop at a muddy parking lot, and nothing happens for a long while, except the cry of an animal far away, an answering thunderbolt. The vehicle has space for a dozen passengers, but she is alone. It feels more graceful to be alone. She is certain Kadeja and the others had to share breaths, glances, sounds they would have wished to keep to themselves. But grace can be terrifying in its vastness.

Finally the men circle round to the back and let her out. She sees a leviathan of shipping containers stacked high, making a boundary for the landscape of grey nothingness.

Lily's limbs are free, but she does not try to run. This time, there is no scene to make, no games to play. Hands on her shoulders guide her to a rust-red container, and other hands open its heavy padlock.

'Enjoy your stay,' one of the men says, pushing her into the dark.

It takes a while to realise just how dark it is, and how hot, even when there are no others to share the air. There are many others, but they do not breathe anymore.

Time passes, and it remains dark enough that Lily does not have to know if she would recognise their faces. This is a small blessing.

She cannot remember how long it takes to die from dehydration. She curls up into a foetal position on the floor, feeling the pattern on the sheet metal bite into her skin. Her hands brush the bruises on her face, reminding her of Mia's fingers on her jawbone, the pure desire to hurt she'd seen in her eyes. It is a beautiful memory, but she can only keep replaying it for so long until it starts fraying around the edges. Lily dreams of a crystal gun, sweet trigger release. There is no strip of film running before her eyes. Memory is a bad director, blind drunk and evil. All scenes disjointed, distorted into something that digs deeper the pit of dread in her stomach, fills it with something worse than hollow. The bitterness she deserves. This she does not –

At some point the hinges open again, and Lily catches a glimpse of a blinding sky, a face at least half-divine to her.

'No,' Lily whispers.

Their faces are wet in the darkness, all boundaries disappearing. Their eyes closed, both of them find themselves in a womb, that dark sea flooding back in.

Acknowledgements

Lisa & Alice, for believing in this novel.

Max & Nour, for reading earlier drafts of this story and helping me figure out what I was grasping through the dark. You are very dear to me.

My sister, for still being here. Olet rakas.

Bart/Wen Long, for being patient with me every day, making me endless cups of coffee and teaching me about dialogue and dramaturgy. I want to make your light blue dreams come true, and the jade green one too. 我爱你。